Seducing the Boss Lady

Sharon C. Cooper

Seducing the Boss Lady
By: Sharon C. Cooper

ISBN: 978-0-9976141-1-4
Book Cover: Selestiele Designs
Editor: Yolanda Barber -Write Time, Write Place
Formatted by: Enterprise Book Services, LLC
Published by: Amaris Publishing LLC in the United
States

Disclaimer

About the series:

Dear Reader

I enjoy reading books that are a part of a series, and now I find that I enjoy writing them as well. Join me as I introduce you to a few members of the Jenkins family.

Steven Jenkins, the patriarch of the Jenkins family, and founder of Jenkins & Sons Construction wants what every entrepreneur head of the family wants - for his children to continue to run the family business long after he's dead and gone. None of his four sons and three daughters are interested in taking over the reins. It's not until his oldest granddaughter, Peyton Jenkins, shows an interest that his hope is renewed.

Now its 16 years later, he's happily retired, and business is better than ever - thanks to his five amazing granddaughters. Toni (TJ) Jenkins, a master plumber, is his favorite granddaughter - though he'll never admit it; Jada (JJ) Jenkins is the youngest and the most spirited of the bunch. Steven still hasn't been able to figure her out, but he has to admit, she's a darn good sheet metal worker. Then there's Christina (CJ) Jenkins, the shy one in the group and the most compassionate. She's a painter, but refers to herself as an artist. Martina (MJ) Jenkins, is a carpenter and Steven's most challenging grandchild who keeps everyone on their toes. Last, but not least, is sweet, levelheaded Peyton (PJ) Jenkins - an electrician and the senior construction manager for Jenkins & Sons Construction.

This is Peyton Jenkins story. Enjoy!

Chapter One

"Excuse me. Pardon me." Peyton Jenkins' breaths came in short spurts as she ran through the airport in three-inch-heels, pulling her small carry-on bag behind her. She held a cell phone to her ear with her other hand as she darted between people, praying she wouldn't miss her connecting flight to Jamaica.

"Okay, MJ. Gotta go." Peyton slowed to dig into the side pocket of her Coach bag in search of her boarding pass. She needed to double-check the gate number. "Oh and don't worry, I won't call again."

"See that you don't. And PJ, try to have some fun for a change. Let your hair down, and I mean that literally," Martina Jenkins-Kendricks said through the phone line. Leave it to her cousin, who also happened to be her best friend, to do what she usually did — say whatever was on her mind.

Peyton tried to ignore the barb about her hair. So what if she usually wore her shoulder length hair pulled back into a bun at the nape of her neck. That didn't mean she didn't know how to have fun.

"I'm serious, PJ. Enjoy the wedding and consider getting up close and personal with one of those Jamaican men. You can even extend your visit if you find one too irresistible to leave. We have everything covered here," Martina added. "And before you ask, Nick and I are leaving in an hour to meet with the Washington Group about their expansion project. You have nothing to worry about."

Yeah, famous last words, Peyton thought. She knew her cousins could handle the operations of the family business, Jenkins & Sons Construction, but that still didn't stop Peyton from worrying. When her grandfather retired, she became the senior manager and poured her life into making the company a success.

"Okay. I won't worry," she finally said, gate thirty-two looming in the distance. "But don't touch any document on my desk. I have everything in a specific order, and I don't want to have to sort through those papers again when I get back."

"Yeah, yeah, whatever. Just get off the phone and don't call us until you're back in Cincinnati. Bye."

"Okay bye." Peyton dropped the cell phone into the side pocket of her handbag and started running again. She couldn't miss this flight. The next plane to Jamaica wouldn't leave until later that evening, and the last thing she wanted was to sit around Miami International Airport for hours.

She couldn't remember the last time she had taken a vacation. Although, this wasn't exactly the vacation she had in mind. Her sister, Christina and her fiancé, Luke, had decided to have a destination wedding – in Jamaica. And as Christina's maid-of-honor, Peyton had to be there. Actually, even if she wasn't standing up for her sister, there's no way she would miss Christina's wedding.

Just because her own marriage of five years ended bitterly, didn't mean she didn't believe in holy matrimony.

Anger stabbed her in the chest. That's what happened whenever memories of finding her ex-husband and his assistant screwing on the living room sofa, penetrated her mind. For the past three years, his infidelity weighed heavy in her heart. Peyton had given her all to him and their marriage. It hadn't been enough. She hadn't been enough.

She had moved on and was doing okay, or so she thought until recently. Over the last two years, watching each of her cousins fall in love had sent her spiraling into depression. Most days she functioned, barely, but some days she forced herself to climb out of bed to face the world. She worked ridiculously long hours to fill the void that continued to grow in her life.

Just as Peyton arrived at the gate, the airport personnel started closing the door.

"Wait!" she screamed. "Please, wait. I'm here. I'm here."

"You just made it," the woman said.

Peyton's chest heaved. "Th…Thank you." She showed her boarding pass and then hurried down the breezeway toward the airplane.

"Good morning, glad you made it," a perky flight attendant with blond hair and heavy eye makeup greeted. "Do you need help with your bag? Most of the overhead bins are full, but yours is fairly small. I might be able to find a spot."

"Thanks, but it'll fit under the seat in front of me."

Peyton didn't feel much like smiling or showing herself friendly. All she wanted to do was find her seat, close her eyes, and sleep for the entire flight. Thanks to Christina, who had gifted her with the trip, including first class seats, she should have a comfortable flight.

Peyton glanced at the boarding pass in her hand to confirm her row and seat. *4A*.

Annoyance jockeyed within her. Of course, someone would be sitting in *4A* because that's the way her morning had been going. First getting to the office at three and losing track of time, then running for her first flight only to be told once she was on the plane that it was delayed. Then landing in Miami thirty minutes late and having to run through yet another airport.

"Excuse me. You're in my seat," Peyton said to the man who was on his cell phone, papers and a file folder spread across the seat near the window as if he owned the whole row, using it as his office. "*Excuse me*," she said a little louder when he ignored her.

Finally, he glanced up.

Peyton's breath caught, and she swallowed hard. Hypnotic, light-brown, almost hazel-colored eyes met hers and she struggled to keep her mouth from hanging open. The man's eyes, such a startling contrast against his tawny brown skin, stood out like a beacon in the night, guiding a lost soul home.

His intense gaze started at her slicked back hair and did a leisure crawl down her body, taking in every inch of her until he reached her black pumps. Suddenly, Peyton wished she had dressed a little sexier. Those gorgeous eyes met hers again, and her pulse kicked up. He didn't speak, didn't smile, nothing. But it was as if a magnetic force passed between them, his scrutiny pulling her in as he studied her face and she studied his.

Peyton's throat went dry as she stood motionless.

"I'm sorry, ma'am, but we need you to take your seat." The flight attendant slammed closed the bin above Peyton's head.

Poof. The spell was broken.

"And sir, I'm going to have to ask you to put your cell phone away as we prepare for takeoff."

Peyton straightened and finally found her voice again. "You're in my seat."

"Brandee, I have to go," Mr. Gorgeous Eyes said into his cell phone, his attention steady on Peyton. "You should have enough work to keep you busy until I get back."

He disconnected his call, and Peyton watched impatiently as he slowly gathered the papers from the seat next to him, stuffing them into a black messenger bag. Normally she wasn't one to make a big deal over a seat assignment, especially in first class, but flying already wigged her out and a seat next to the window made the experience worse.

The guy didn't seem to care that she was standing in the aisle waiting for him. He continued to take his time, giving her the chance to check him out. Though his hair was neat and cut low, he had at least a day's growth of hair shadowing his cheek, chin and just above his lip. Peyton had always been attracted to men with a little scruff. And this guy possessed a bit of a bad-boy vibe. His broad shoulders with muscular arms, bunched beneath his long sleeved, fitted T-shirt each time he moved. Her gaze took in his wide chest and flat abs, moving down...

Peyton blinked several times. Had it been that long since she'd been with a man that she was visually drooling over a perfect stranger? Maybe Martina was right. Maybe it was time to let her hair down. Putting in twenty-hour days, burying herself in work, she hadn't been with a man since...since forever.

Mr. Gorgeous Eyes stood. Peyton hadn't realized how

tall he was, at least six feet. Her senses came alive when his woodsy fragrance with a hint of ginger, drifted past her nose as he stepped into the aisle.

Hold up. Wait. Why was he in the aisle, acting as if he was waiting for her to slide into the window seat?

"I think there's been some misunderstanding. I have the aisle seat," she said.

"There must be a mistake, sweetheart," Gorgeous Eyes said, his smooth, deep voice just as awe-inspiring as his eyes. "I always get the aisle seat. So if this is your row, you must have the window seat."

The frustration swirling in Peyton's gut upon entering the airplane had now changed to anger and nipped at her last nerve. "Well, I guess there is a mistake – on your part – *sweetheart*. I have the aisle seat." She shoved her boarding pass in front of his face, placing her finger next to the seat assignment. "So if you'll slide in or find somewhere else to sit, I'd appreciate it."

He hesitated and then cursed under his breath. "Tell you what," he dug through one of his front pants pockets and pulled out a thin wallet, "I'll give you two hundred dollars to let me keep the aisle seat, and you take the window."

He waved two crisp, one hundred dollar bills in her face, an I-can-get-whatever-the-hell-I-want grin on his lips.

Revulsion clawed at her insides, and Peyton glared at him. It had been a long time since she wanted to punch someone for trying to take advantage of her. The last person had been her ex-husband. She didn't need another good-looking, arrogant man who thought he could sweet-talk her, or in this case, buy her off to get what he wanted. "I don't want your damn money!"

The man's left brow rose a fraction at her outburst,

and she glanced away realizing they had garnered attention from nearby passengers. Some sipped wine, glancing at them over their drinking glasses, whereas others stared openly.

Why couldn't this day get better instead of worse? Since opening her eyes and climbing out of bed, there had been one situation after another. All she wanted to do was get to Jamaica in one piece and relax on the beach without any drama.

Blowing out a breath, a second passed before Peyton returned her attention to the irritating man.

"I don't know who you think you are," she leaned in and spoke in a low, controlled voice though she felt anything but, her heart hammering in her chest. "You can't just buy people off." Everything about the man wreaked delicious havoc on her senses. Those eyes that seemed to take in every aspect of her, studied her, and then a crooked smile tilted the left side of his tempting lips. Lips so inviting that if she took heed of Martina's suggestion of having a good time while on vacation, Peyton could start with him. She had no doubt she would enjoy kissing him.

Still holding the money up, he said, "I'm sorry. I'm not trying to upset you. It's just that my legs are too long and—"

"Ma'am, sir, we need you both to take your seats. We can't take off until everyone is seated."

"I would if he would quit messing around and slide in. I have the aisle seat." Peyton held her boarding pass up for the flight attendant to examine, her patience totally spent.

"She's right, sir. Now if you both can take a seat, we can get going."

"Last chance, sweetheart." He waved the money in

front of her. "I don't offer just anyone this much money."

"Don't call me sweetheart and just so you know, I don't take money from just anyone," she said through gritted teeth. "Oh and another thing. This is *your* last chance. Once I sit in that seat right there, you're going to have to get to the window seat the best way you can."

He chuckled and hesitated again as if thinking she was kidding. When she didn't move, he eventually entered the row and moved to the window. "You're cold, woman. Just cold."

"Arrogant ass," she murmured.

Once Peyton shoved her small purse and laptop bag under the seat in front of her, she quickly fastened the seatbelt. This was going to be a long flight. Not only was the man next to her full of himself and too darn good-looking for his own good, but his enchanting scent compelled her to want to lean in and get a better whiff.

How could someone who looked and smelled as good as he did, be such a jerk? How dare he offer her money.

Your ass should have taken the cash. The sound of Martina's voice invaded Peyton's mind, and she almost smiled. Her cousin, the hothead in the family, would have given the man a verbal tongue lashing had she been there. She would have also taken his money and not given up the seat.

Gorgeous Eyes rubbed his hands down his jean-clad thighs and Peyton tried to force herself to look away, but she couldn't. If those large hands hadn't caught her attention, his thick thighs would have. He undoubtedly spent time in a gym, perfecting that body and flexing so the gym bunnies could stroke his over-inflated ego.

Peyton shook her head, trying to clear thoughts of him. What was wrong with her? She didn't even know the guy, yet was judging him based on their seat issue. Then again, the tacky offer of money didn't help his case.

The airplane backed away from the gate and the flight attendant at the front of the plane gave the routine safety information. Though Peyton could almost recite the spiel by heart, she tried listening. Just in case. Just in case the plane went down and she had to act fast, but the man next to her was a distraction she couldn't seem to ignore.

Gorgeous Eyes turned to her. "I'm sorry about the seat situation. Maybe we can start over. I'm Michael Cutter...the arrogant ass."

Oh crap. Heat rose to Peyton's cheek, and she slid down a little in her seat. Had she said that out loud? Sure, she meant it, but she hadn't planned on actually calling him that to his face.

"Peyton Jenkins," she mumbled her name wishing she could crawl under a boulder.

The airplane roared down the runway and Peyton's heart stuttered. She gripped the armrest, and her body tensed from the top of her head to the tip of her toes, her pulse pounding in her ear.

"Are you afraid of flying?" Gorgeous Eyes laid his hand over hers, and she yanked out of his grasp, narrowing her eyes at him.

"Just because I told you my name doesn't mean I'm not pissed at you. Nor does it mean I want to have a conversation with you."

The plane took off, and Peyton sucked in a breath, her eyes tightly closed. Just breathe. In and out. In and out. The words looped through her mind as she tried not to focus on the fact that they were going to be soaring through the sky at 160 miles an hour, thirty thousand feet into the air.

"Relax," Michael said covering her hand again. This

time she didn't shake him off. "You're as tense as a porcupine in a balloon factory."

"What?" Her eyes popped open. "That doesn't even make sense. If anything is going to be tense, it would be a balloon in a porcupine factory," she said, adding her two cents to the stupid conversation.

"Okay, a balloon in a porcupine factory, but you get my point. You're too tense. Try to think about something other than flying."

"Like?"

"Like that you turned down two hundred dollars from a very handsome man who was willing to pay more for your seat."

"You really are an arrogant ass aren't you?"

He burst out laughing, and the sound sent warmth through Peyton's body. That along with his crooked grin only enhanced his attractiveness. Irritation soared through her veins at the thought that she found his laugh sexy. And it was a little hard to stay mad at a man who had eyes as warm as a roaring fire on a cold, winter's night.

Still laughing, Michael pulled out his wallet and inserted the bills. "Sorry if I pissed you off. I really did think I had the aisle seat, but apparently my assistant goofed."

Peyton was proud of herself for not falling for this guy's good looks or his charm. Any other time, she would have given up her seat to keep the peace.

"And I didn't mean to offend you with the money. I know I can be a jerk sometimes."

"Well, it's good you know that," Peyton said, and he laughed again. She studied him, zoning in on the dimple in his right cheek. How had she missed that cute indent until now? She noticed his full, kissable lips and the cleft in his chin, but she had also missed the jagged, five-inch scar marring his neck.

They leaned back in their seats and Peyton realized Michael had distracted her while the plane leveled off.

Okay, maybe he wasn't such a bad guy.

*

Michael Cutter couldn't stop the smile from spreading across his face. Maybe his first impression of this woman had been wrong. Hair pulled severely back from her face and bound at the back of her neck, wearing a plain V-neck blouse and dark slacks, she definitely had that librarian or maybe a preschool teacher thing going on. Her sharp tongue said otherwise. He liked the way she stood her ground and called him out over offering her money. The woman had sass. He liked sass.

A former New York City cop and now a private investigator, he usually could size up individuals at first glance. Not this woman. No doubt she was beautiful, but the way she downplayed her looks only meant one thing. She was hiding. Not necessarily from something or someone, but from who she really was. And then there was the sadness that flickered in her eyes when she wasn't scowling at him. What was her story?

He turned back to Peyton. Cute name. It suited her. Despite her eyes being closed, he was sure she hadn't fallen asleep yet, but probably determined to tune him out. His gaze took in her flawless cafe au lait skin, slowing at her glossed lips before going lower to her more than a handful, perky breasts. She wasn't fat, but wasn't skinny either, just the way he...

Whoa!

Michael shook his head as if the move would wipe the thought from his mind. He was traveling to Jamaica for not only his best friend's wedding, but also to relax and regroup. Most importantly, he was taking a break from women. He didn't need the headache, even if the headache was as cute as the one sitting next to him.

Michael pulled *Motor Cyclist* from his bag and flipped the magazine open. He barely got to page two before he stole another glance at his seatmate. She seemed more relaxed now that the plane had leveled off. Her eyes were closed, and her long lashes brushed the top of her high cheekbones. Her skin was flawless, with very little makeup and…

"Are you planning to stare at me the entire flight?" she asked, her eyes still closed.

"Are you going to continue to pretend to be asleep to keep me from talking to you?"

Normally when he flew, he kept to himself, reviewed case notes, or caught up on some reading. However, there was something about this woman that piqued his interest.

"I'm not pretending to sleep. I'm resting my eyes, hoping to fall asleep, but you keep looking at me. Besides, you're distr…"

His brow lifted. "I'm what? I'm sitting here, minding my own business, trying to read my magazine. You're the one who's acting all…"

"What?" She opened her eyes and turned to him. "Acting like what? Say it."

A grin pulled at his lips. "You're attracted to me aren't you? And my presence is inflicting turbulence through your body isn't it?"

It took everything within him not to burst out laughing at the scowl covering her gorgeous face.

"Oh my God, you're too much." She dropped back in her seat and closed her eyes again, shaking her head. "You're just too much."

This time Michael did burst out laughing. "I thought I was an arrogant ass."

"That too."

Her smart retorts just didn't match her uptight, straight-laced persona. Too bad he was taking a break from women. Otherwise, he would find out where she was staying on the island and ask her out to dinner. Then again, maybe it was best to leave well enough alone.

He reopened his magazine and settled in for the rest of the ride. Yep, best to leave well enough alone.

Chapter Two

Peyton fumbled with her luggage, dragging the bags out of the airport, hurrying to catch the shuttle that would take her to Ocho Rios.

"Wait. Wait, I'm here!" She trotted to the back of the shuttle van, where the driver was just about to close the door. "I'm sorry."

He accepted her bags and loaded them on. "No problem."

Peyton climbed onto the bus and did a quick glance around. *Full.* Frustration gnawed on her last nerve. Of course, all of the seats would be taken, because that's the type of day she was having.

She eased down the aisle toward the back. Several steps in, she stopped. Her gaze met Michael's. Like earlier, heat engulfed her body at the sight of him. What was it about this man that made everything within her come alive?

He slowly unfolded his body and stood in the aisle. He waved his hand toward the inside seat next to him, but her feet wouldn't move. Sitting next to him on the plane for the last couple of hours had been enough. Any more time with this guy and she might do something stupid like climb into his lap and taste the lips she dreamed about after dozing off on the plane.

Nope. No way was she going to embarrass herself. Just then, a man two rows in front of her stood.

"Here's an empty seat." He pointed to his row. Peyton took him in. He had to be at least 300 pounds and sweaty as if the air conditioning on the bus wasn't working. She groaned inside not liking either choice at the moment.

After a slight hesitation, Peyton accepted the seat next to Big Man. A quick glance down the aisle showed Michael, his brows lifted in surprise.

Good. She had knocked him down a peg or two, hurling him off that self-created pedestal. Served him right for grating on her nerves earlier. Though she had managed to nap off and on during the flight, her body was so aware of him, more aware than it had been with any man lately.

Peyton took her seat. Now, if she could forget that she and Michael ever met and survive the next hour and a half without getting squashed by Big Man spilling over into her seat, then maybe she could get in another nap.

*

What the hell?

Michael reclaimed his seat shocked that out of the only two available seats, Peyton chose to sit with the man who clearly needed the whole row.

I must be losing my touch.

She saw that he was offering the seat next to him but dissed him anyway. Maybe she was still ticked about the situation on the airplane.

Fine. Good riddance.

Michael settled in for the long ride, resting against the

headrest and glad Peyton decided to sit somewhere else. He had enjoyed having her snuggled up, sleeping next to him a little too much on the plane. He was officially on vacation. The last thing he needed was to complicate his time off by having his mind hijacked with thoughts of the beautiful woman who thought he was an arrogant ass.

A smile played around his mouth. He'd been called worse. But hearing the words from her was funny considering she looked like the type who never cursed and always followed the rules. So unlike most women he found himself attracted to – edgy with straight-up attitude.

His eyes popped open, and he straightened. Why the hell was he even thinking about the woman?

He glanced at Peyton. Michael didn't know what she and her seatmate were discussing, but whatever the conversation was about, had her leaning away and frowning at the man.

Unease crawled up Michael's spine. The closer the guy leaned in, the more Peyton tried to back away with nowhere to go.

Michael looked away. It wasn't his business what they were discussing or how creeped out she seemed. She had made her choice.

Just mind your own business.

Michael had never been good at minding his own business – especially when it came to a woman being mistreated. He still had the wounds to prove it. He rubbed the long scar on his neck, a reminder of what happened the last time he stepped in to play hero.

"Hey!" Peyton's voice reached Michael, and she shoved the guy next to her. As if there was a string that connected him to her, Michael was out of his seat before he could stop himself.

*

"Come on. Why are you playing hard to get?" Big Man persisted, leaning close again, his breath hot on the side of Peyton's face. "Have dinner with me."

"I'm not interested," she repeated for what felt like the hundredth time.

"Why not?" His brows drew together, confusion covering his face as if he couldn't believe she was actually turning him down.

It wasn't in Peyton's nature to be mean to anyone, but this idiot...

"What part of not interested don't you understand?"

"So how long are you going to stay mad at me?"

Peyton's gaze jerked up and landed on Michael, who was standing in the aisle. He held onto the seat in front of them, the shuttle swaying back and forth, bouncing around on rugged terrain.

"What? I...I," was all Peyton could get out as her mouth opened, closed and opened again, not sure what to think of his question.

"Get lost," Big Man said to Michael, surprising Peyton. What surprised her more was the glacial glint in Michael's eyes. A sudden dangerous air about him sent a shiver spiraling through her. For a moment, she wondered if she weren't better off staying next to Big Man.

"I'm not leaving without her," Michael said and extended his hand. The gentleness Peyton now witnessed in his eyes was like earlier. Like when he held her hand, distracting her during the airplane's takeoff. "Come on. You can be mad at me later." She grabbed his hand as if she were reaching for a life rafter in the middle of the ocean.

"Excuse me," Peyton mumbled when she realized she

couldn't cross in front of her seatmate.

The man hesitated, and then struggled to stand, his girth blocking her path requiring him to step further into the aisle.

Michael stepped back and pulled Peyton against the front of his body, sending jolts of electricity shooting to the soles of her feet. Sweat beaded along her hairline at their closeness, and she wished Big Man would hurry the hell up and get out of the way.

The moment the aisle was clear again, Peyton scurried away from Michael and hurried to his row, finally able to breathe. She dropped down in the seat and slouched, hoping that they hadn't made too much of a scene.

God please. No more issues. Just get me to the resort without any more drama.

"You're welcome," Michael said.

Peyton glanced at him. Again he wore that stupid, smug, I-can-get-anything-I-want grin. Clearly he was proud of himself. She wanted to ignore him and be mad that he had butted in. She couldn't. Instead, she felt the urge to throw her arms around his neck and kiss him in gratitude.

She mentally shook herself. There would be no kissing, or touching for that matter. "Thanks," she finally said loud enough for only him to hear.

His brows bunched together. "Thanks? That's it? Just thanks?" His volume matched hers. To anyone else they probably looked like a couple having a lovers' spat.

"What do you want me to say? It's not like you really did anything."

"Are you kidding me? You could sound a little more appreciative. I just saved your cute little ass from being squashed by that Sasquatch."

He thinks I'm cute? Wait a minute. Who cared what he

thought? He might be gorgeous and smelled amazing, but still. Peyton stayed clear of men like him. *Too* good looking, confident with a take-charge, and a holier-than-thou attitude. Unfortunately, that was also the type of men who caught her attention.

She might've been feeling lonely lately, but not lonely enough to hook up with another man like her ex-husband. She'd already had a hot, arrogant, selfish man in her life. The next time around, assuming there would be a next time, she wanted someone who cherished and respected her.

But right now, sitting so close to Michael, she could barely think straight. It was bad enough she had to sit next to him earlier. By the time they had deplaned, her body had been tingling in ways she hadn't experienced in a long time. He was a stranger. Still, there was something about him that...

Nope. She wasn't going there. Besides, after today, she would never see him again.

"If nothing else, you should at least be thanking me that I let you sit next to me."

Peyton rolled her eyes. "Whatever. It's not like I can't take care of myself. I didn't ask you to intervene."

She turned and stared out the window. As the oldest of her two siblings and most of her cousins, it seemed she had also been taking care of those around her. It was actually kind of nice to have someone come to her rescue, even if it was the arrogant ass.

"If you can take care of yourself, you wouldn't have looked like a turkey about to be slaughtered when that guy came on to you."

Apparently, he had seen everything. "What's it to you? Is your conscience bothering you? You insult me earlier by offering me money, now you want to redeem yourself

19

by coming to my rescue."

He didn't respond. A vulnerable glint sparked in his eyes but was gone just as quickly as it had appeared.

What was that look? What had she said to render him speechless?

"Michael?"

"You're right. Anything involving you is none of my business. Sorry I interfered," he said, his tone signaling the end of the discussion.

They'd spent the last few hours together, and this was the first hint of a serious side. Earlier he'd said any and everything to get her attention, but now he seemed different.

"I'm sorry for snapping at you. I do appreciate you stepping in."

"No problem." He shifted in his seat, his arms folded across his chest. He closed his eyes, effectively tuning her out.

Way to go, Peyton.

She studied his profile. He appeared to be asleep, but the hard set of his jaw indicated otherwise.

Peyton sighed and stared out the window again. It was just as well. Had they kept talking, he probably would have said something else to drive her nuts.

Before long, her eyes grew heavy, and she succumbed to fatigue.

"Peyton." Someone was shaking her shoulder. "Peyton."

Peyton jerked awake, her head turning left then right before the fog of sleep lifted, and she zoned in on Michael towering over her.

"Hey. I'm not sure where you're headed, but this is my stop. I figured I'd wake you before—"

"This is my stop," she said in a rush when she looked

past him out the window. Her sister, Christina, and Luke were standing in front of the resort.

"You're staying here?" Michael asked.

That's when Peyton realized they were staying at the same place. Instead of responding, she nodded and moved past him.

"Well, surprises never cease," Michael mumbled as they stepped off the shuttle.

"Hey, you guys!" Christina Jenkins ran over and hugged Peyton before hugging Michael. "I see you two have met."

"Wait."

"What?"

Peyton and Michael spoke at once, glancing at each other before splitting their attention between Christina and Luke.

"What's going on? You know him?" Peyton asked Christina, pointing at Michael.

"Mike and I go way back." Luke and Michael embraced, clapping each other on the back. The adoration and brotherly bond between the men couldn't be missed. "Mike is one of my best friends."

"And Peyton is my sister," Christina said to Michael.

You've got to be kidding me, Peyton thought. She was attracted to a man who she thought she would never see again. A man she hoped to never see again. Yet, here they were at the same resort. Participants in the same wedding.

"Mike is one of the best private investigators in New York City." Christina looped her arm through Peyton's. "I assumed you two had met since you got off the bus together and...oh never mind. I need to talk to you." She pulled on Peyton's arm, dragging her away from the guys. "I'm so glad you're here."

"Me too."

Sharon C. Cooper

Peyton slipped on her sunglasses. Though she hadn't wanted to take off of work, she was glad to be in Jamaica and looked forward to soaking up the sunshine.

Christina maintained the hold on Peyton's arm, moving at least twenty feet from the shuttle. The hugger of the family, she could best be described as a free-spirited flower child. From her save-the-world attitude, to her style of dress, like now wearing a tie-dye T-shirt and long prairie-style skirt, Christina was one of the sweetest people Peyton knew.

"Wait." Peyton stopped. "I almost forgot. Let me grab my luggage."

"Luke will take care of your bags." Christina pulled her further away from the guys.

"Okay, what's going on?" Peyton asked when Christina stopped and stood in front of her, her hands gripping Peyton's upper arms.

"We have a situation."

"Oh no. Tell me nothing happened to your dress." Peyton went immediately into fix-it mode. Something she did on a daily basis either at work or with the Jenkins family. "Don't worry. Whatever it is, we can fix it. We have time to find you anoth—"

"It's nothing like that, except, the resort did have to change the spot of where we wanted to get married, to another location on the property. There was some schedule mix-up."

"What? That's crazy. What if you and Luke had your hearts set on that particular spot?"

"Oh please. You know it's not that serious to us. I'm getting married in paradise and marrying the man of my dreams. Besides, all of the wedding locations on the property are amazing."

Peyton yawned, ready to crawl into bed and sleep the

rest of the day away. "Okay, so if you're okay with the new wedding location, what's the problem? Why'd you pull me over here?"

Peyton glanced at Luke and Michael, noting their heated exchanged and Michael jabbing Luke in the chest with his finger. Her gaze journeyed down Michael's athletic build and how the long-sleeved T-shirt hugged his biceps and laid flat against his abs. Looked as though he had traveled from a cold-weather climate based on the way he was dressed. His jeans hung low, and the way the pant legs stuck partially in a pair of black Timberland boots made him appear tough and sexy. Peyton had always been attracted to ruggedly handsome men and Michael definitely fit the bill.

Still, she wondered about their spirited discussion. Luke, a defense attorney, didn't back down from anyone. But he was taking a serious tongue-lashing from Michael.

Peyton returned her attention to Christina. Michael wasn't her concern, and she'd do well to remember that.

"CJ, can whatever you have to tell me wait? It's hot out here. I just want to check in, go to my room, and sleep for a few hours in the air conditioning."

"Well, you see, here's the thing."

Peyton stiffened. Apprehension nipped at her nerves and the hairs on the back of her neck stood at attention. Another glance at the guys and Peyton knew she wasn't going to like whatever her sister had to say. Bad news was coming. That would explain why Christina and Luke were standing out front when Peyton arrived.

"CJ, if you tell me that you or Toni screwed up my reservation, so help me, I'm going to strangle you."

Christina chuckled, pushing her long curly hair away from her face. "You've been hanging around MJ too much. That sounds like something she would say."

"I'm not playing. I'm too tired for games. Just tell me what's going on."

"Okay, so this resort is for couples only and all of our guests are coupled up except…"

Silence fell between them, and Peyton was glad her sunglasses shielded her eyes. "Except for me," she whispered. Sadness lodged inside her heart as tears pricked the back of her eyes. Same old story. Once again she was the odd man out, the one lacking a man on her arm.

Peyton turned away from Christina, wrapped her arms around herself, and glanced at the surroundings for the first time since stepping off the bus. A large, water fountain sat on the front lawn of the resort, colorful flowers around the base.

Despite leaving forty-degree weather in Cincinnati, it had to be at least eighty degrees in Ocho Rios and maybe even warmer under the vibrant sun. Palm trees swayed slightly in the light breeze that kissed her face, doing nothing to help the humidity that had her blouse sticking to her back. And the smooth sound of drums and a man singing in the distance should have made her look forward to her stay, but instead made her sadder.

Peyton's chest tightened. Disappointment and exhaustion was starting to get the best of her. One by one, her cousins were finding their significant others. Though happy for all of them, there were times when Peyton found it difficult to watch them play kissy face with their men. In Cincinnati, she could bury herself in work, but this weekend, with all of them there, love would be in the air. And she would be the only one not paired up.

Three years divorced, it wasn't that she didn't want to fall in love and try marriage again. No, Peyton wanted nothing more than to meet a nice guy, get married and possibly have a family. But her chances for a happily-ever-after looked bleaker by the day. Besides, she didn't know if she would ever be able to trust a man with her heart again.

"I'm sorry, sis." Christina placed her arm around Peyton's shoulder. "Luke and I decided to get married here because they offered Wedding-moons. It wasn't until later that I found out the resort was for couples only and by then I had fallen in love with all that the resort offered."

"Well, what am I supposed to do, CJ?" Peyton shook out of Christina's grasp. "You should have told me sooner. At least then I could have made reservations somewhere else."

"I made you a reservation...here."

Peyton snatched off her shades and glared at Christina. "You just said the resort is for couples only. How... What have you done?" Peyton asked through gritted teeth, barely able to contain her anger.

"I...uh. I kinda coupled you up with someone."

"Who? I know everyone who's coming, and everyone has some..." Peyton's words died on her tongue as realization dawned on her. "No!" She backed away from Christina before her sister grabbed hold of her arm.

"PJ, wait. Just hear me out."

"No! Christina, you have done some crazy things in your life, but this...this... How could you do this to me?" she choked out. It was bad enough her cousins had tried setting her up on pity dates over the last few years, but this was unbelievable. "How could you?"

"Sis, please don't cry. It's all going to work out fine. Mike is a sweetheart."

"I don't know him, CJ. You're asking me to live with a

man for the next few days, who I know nothing about. What will mom and dad think about me sharing a room with some stranger? And don't even get me started about what Gram is going to say. You know how she feels about shacking up."

Christina waved her off. "Mom and Dad aren't going to judge you. As for Gramma and Grampa, they're not even going to know who you're staying with and probably won't realize it's a resort for couples. Besides, you're grown. It's nobody's business what you do or who you decide to do it with."

Unlike Christina and their mother, who walked around as if all was well with the world, Peyton always followed the rules. Respected rules. Predictable. Unfortunately, she lived her life as a people pleaser, caring what others thought and tried never to make trouble. Just once, she would like to throw caution out the window, enjoy life for a change, and have some new experiences, but not like this.

"Peyton, you need to stop worrying about what others think. Try to have a little fun."

If one more person said that to her, she was going to scream.

"I'm not telling you to sleep with Mike, but you could do a lot worse."

Anxiety bounced around inside of Peyton, and she closed her eyes. Rubbing her forehead, she wasn't sure what to do.

"As for Mike, I'll tell you anything you want to know about him. Or better yet, get to know him yourself. You have a full day to learn all there is to know about him before everyone else gets here tomorrow. Just please, don't be mad."

Peyton's eyes popped open. "Don't be mad? Are you

for real?" she spat. "I'm mad as hell! If I weren't so tired and if there was a chance that I could get a flight out, I'd be on the next plane back to Cincinnati."

"Now you're overreacting, PJ."

Her sister's words only made Peyton angrier. "You know what? I'll find someplace else to stay. There have to be plenty of resorts nearby where I can get a room."

"Luke already checked. All the hotels and resorts are booked within a ten-mile radius. Colleges are on spring break."

Peyton didn't know if Christina was telling the truth or not. All Peyton knew was that her heart pounded faster than a locomotive flying down a track, and at any second someone would have to pull her off of Christina. At thirty-five, six years older than Christina, Peyton couldn't ever remember them having a physical fight, but there was a first time for everything.

"Come on, PJ. Don't be mad. I'm sorry."

"Sorry isn't going to cut it this time, Christina. I don't know if I'll ever forgive you for putting me in this position."

Chapter Three

"I think your woman has made you lose your damn mind!" Michael growled at Luke. "Because clearly you're not thinking straight if you think I'm going to share my room."

"CJ only told me about the resort's stipulations a couple of days ago."

"And your ass couldn't pick up the damn phone and let me know before today?"

"No, because then you would've brought a date. And CJ didn't want Peyton to have to find some other place to stay."

"Luke, are you listening to yourself? I'm sure if Peyton had known ahead of time, like me, she would have brought a date."

Luke shook his head. "Nah, man, she wouldn't have brought anyone. I've known her a long time. I have never seen Peyton with a man. Unlike you, I doubt she could have found someone on such short notice."

Michael still couldn't believe Peyton and Christina were sisters. He'd met Luke's fiancée on a few occasions whenever they visited New York, and Christina had often talked about her sister, the boss lady.

Michael had spent most of the morning with Peyton. He would never have guessed she and Christina were related. They might have favored each other, but they were clearly as different as apples and oranges. Christina was a free-spirit to the bone, willing to walk on the wild side whenever an opportunity presented itself. Peyton, from the little he knew about her, was Christina's polar opposite.

"So I'm supposed to share my room and my mini-vacation with a woman I just met?"

Luke chuckled. "It's not like you haven't done it before. Remember Melissa in the Bahamas? Or what about that woman you met when we flew out to LA a couple of years ago? What was her name? Leslie or—"

"Those situations were different. Hell, I was different. Besides, I already know Peyton is not that type of woman."

Michael glanced over his shoulder at Christina and Peyton, who were in a heated discussion. It looked as though Peyton wasn't taking the news any better than he had. They were too far away for him to hear the conversation, but he noticed the way she kept swiping at her eyes.

Michael ran a hand over his head and let it slide down to the back of his neck. "I don't need any shit this weekend, and you already know how I feel about living under the same roof with a woman. I don't like putting myself in that type of situation."

Luke gripped Michael's shoulder, forcing him to meet his friend's gaze. "When are you going to start listening to me? You are nothing like Lewis. You're one of the good guys who always treats women with respect. Besides there is no way in hell, I would go along with this harebrained idea of CJ's if I thought you would cause physical harm to my future sister-in-law. My only concern now is that she might fall for your charming ass."

Michael shook his head and chuckled, appreciating his friend's ability to lighten the moment. "Don't worry. I have no intention of seducing the boss lady."

"On a serious note, Mike, you have to stop letting one incident dictate how you live the rest of your life."

"You know it's not just that one incident that has me being careful where women are concerned."

"I know, but it was after the bar incident that you changed. That situation happened almost nine years ago, yes it was a hella crazy time, but you survived it."

Michael rubbed the scar on his neck. He had moved on, but he would never forget that night for as long as he lived. "Yeah, thanks to you. I don't even want to think about where my life would be if you hadn't saved my ass."

"Let the past go and move on, man. Besides, I think you're going to like Peyton."

"I'm not tryin' to like anybody. I'm tryin' to take a break from the whole dating scene."

Luke's left eyebrow lifted. "As in taking a vow of celibacy?"

"I didn't say all of that," Michael mumbled, stealing another glance at Peyton. Though she was a beautiful woman with big brown eyes and pouty, kissable lips, she wasn't his type. He tended to date taller women, and Peyton couldn't have been more than 5'4 or 5'5. She also seemed a little too stiff and straight-laced for his taste. Too matronly. But he had a feeling that if she got rid of the bun and showed a little more skin, she would definitely turn a few heads.

"So what do you mean you're taking a break?"

Michael shrugged. "I need a break. I'm tired of the same ol' same ol' with these women out here."

Luke remained silent, and Michael knew he had said too much. He could almost hear the gears turning in his friend's enormous brain, forming some unsolicited advice. With a genius level IQ, Luke was the smartest person Michael knew, whether legal jargon or street wisdom, there weren't many subjects he couldn't speak on.

"Maybe you're finally ready to settle down."

"Ha! Yeah, right. That'll never happen. You know my history and since that shit with Lewis and his father, I will never put any woman through some mess like that."

"Mike, man, I'll say it again. You are nothing like your father or your grandfather. How many times do—"

"Drop it, Luke. We're not doing this right now. Besides, if I have to pretend to be a part of a couple, I should probably start now. Peyton looks about ready to pummel your soon-to-be wife. We might as well get this crazy charade started."

"So are we cool?" Luke asked on their way to the women.

"Hell nah, we ain't cool. You're going to owe me big time."

"Would it make you feel better to know that CJ and I are covering your stay?"

"It's a start."

*

"Peyton."

Peyton startled at the sound of Michael's voice behind her. She quickly wiped her face, angry that anyone witnessed her tears. She glared at Christina before turning to him. At least now she knew why he was going off on

31

Luke.

"Michael, I can't—"

"Before you say no," he stepped closer, "hear me out." A jolt of awareness shot through her when Michael's hand went to her hip, pulling her close. "Listen, I don't like this any more than you do," he said near her ear. Peyton assumed he was already getting into character for the few hotel staff lingering nearby. "It's only four nights. Since they reserved a suite, the room should be large enough for us to co-exist without getting in each other's way and I promise I'll be a perfect gentleman."

Peyton glanced up at him, sincerity reigning in his eyes. There was no way her sister would put her in a dangerous situation and Luke had proved over the past year that he was just as protective."

Peyton didn't know if it was defeat, exhaustion or Michael's arresting eyes that had her seriously considering the idea of sharing a room with him. He held her gaze, and she felt her guards slowly lowering. Now she knew why he was conceited. There was just something about this man that had her almost ready to take a walk on the wild side and submit to anything he suggested. Almost.

She swallowed hard and nodded, praying that she wouldn't regret this decision. "Okay, we can pretend we're a couple out in public, but behind closed doors, I'm off limits."

"Alright. You say that now, but I'm pretty irresistible. If you find that *you* can't control yourself around me, feel free to act on your thoughts." He winked.

Peyton rolled her eyes and walked away. "Arrogant ass."

*

After checking in and arranging for their bags to be delivered, Michael and Peyton rode the elevator to their suite in silence. So far, for Michael, the only perk to the situation was that Luke and Christina had taken care of all their resort expenses. He couldn't understand what Luke had been thinking with this setup. Actually, yes he did know. One word: Christina. There was no way his friend would have pulled something like this before she came along, especially without giving him a heads up.

The elevator doors opened, and Michael followed Peyton down the hall. Walking behind her, his gaze traveled the length of her body. From the ridiculous tight bun secured at the back of her head, down to her firm, round butt. She wasn't skinny and definitely not fat. Her hourglass figure was what wet dreams were made of, and he hadn't even seen her naked yet. Maybe the free room and board weren't the only perks to the trip.

"What's the room number again, 1206 or 1208?" Peyton asked, interrupting his thoughts, which were definitely heading in the wrong direction.

He cleared his throat and glanced at the small envelope in his hand that held two access cards. "1202. We should be pretty close."

Peyton stopped at the room door and stepped aside. Her gaze met his for a second before she diverted her attention to the opposite wall, staring as if it held the answers to the universe's most important questions. She was a mix of contradictions and all day, just when Michael thought he had figured her out, a new layer of her personality peeled away. During their travels, she'd been somewhat standoffish at times, but her sass revealed itself whenever she opened her mouth, shining a light on a witty side. Then there was the conversation with her sister. He saw yet another side of her. The tears she had tried hiding, reminded him of the hint of sadness that he'd noticed earlier in those beautiful brown eyes.

Michael inserted the access card, just as a whiff of her enticing floral scent, even more potent than earlier, floated up to his nose. He almost groaned. How the hell was he going to share a room with this woman without loosening her hair bun and stripping her naked?

"Alright, here we are." He pushed the door open.

Peyton crossed the threshold and stopped in the middle of the large living space. "This is gorgeous."

Michael closed the door behind him. From across the room, the ocean came into view through the sliding screen door and the wall of windows. The sounds of waves crashing against the rocks and seagulls squawking nearby pulled him farther into the space, welcoming him to paradise.

Michael tossed the key card to one of the tables near the sofa and gave the room a cursory glance before his attention went back to Peyton. He watched the gentle sway of her hips move to a rhythm all her own as she crossed the terracotta floor and headed straight to the patio door.

Damn.

If Peyton's scent and walk could make his body stir with need, he was in trouble. Instead of following her across the room, he slowed. At that moment, he didn't trust himself to follow her. He always went after what he wanted, and he suddenly wanted this cute little uptight woman who wouldn't hesitate to put him in his place if he stepped out of line. The next few days were going to be hell if he didn't get his libido under control.

"She's not my type," he told himself as he checked out a coat closet and the small kitchenette.

Turning back to the wall of windows and the patio door, his gaze latched on to the view of the ocean. Even from where he stood, he could see the sun's rays glistening off the sparkling blue waters. Peyton leaned on the white railing and drew her head back, soaking up the sun. Finally, it looked as though she was starting to relax.

Michael leaned on the back of one of the upholstered chairs. The tan, striped sofa with two end tables sat on one side of the room and faced a large entertainment center. He took a good look at the space that would probably be his sleeping quarters since they were in a one-bedroom suite.

He shook his head and pushed off of the chair. The day definitely hadn't gone as planned. And what had he been thinking deciding to take a break from women when he knew he would be in Jamaica a few days?

Peyton walked back into the suite and closed the sliding screen door. "This place is truly paradise," she said, releasing the tight bun. "The view out there is breathtaking."

"Yeah, in here too," Michael mumbled, unable to take his gaze off of her, loving the way her hair fell around her shoulders in thick layers. He stood frozen in place as she talked about the white sand, the waves, and the warm weather. And then she smiled.

"This room, the ocean... I don't think four days will be enough. I might have to relocate here."

This was the first time she had actually smiled since being in his presence. The smile transformed her whole face.

Peyton narrowed her eyes at him. "What?" She looked down at herself and then glanced over her shoulder before returning her attention to him. "Why are you looking like that?"

He gave a slight shrug. "Your smile. I think it's the first one I've seen today. It's beautiful. Your face is all lit up, glowing."

Crimson tinted her cheeks. "Oh." She finger-combed her hair oblivious of the effect the move was having on him. He stayed put, ignoring the desire to approach her and run his fingers through the long tresses. "Thank you," she said.

"You're welcome."

Peyton fiddled with the hair band in her hand and Michael waited, sensing she wanted to say more. One thing he had noticed early on is that she wasn't shy. Although the way she hesitated made him think that yet again, he might not have her figured out.

"About what happened on the shuttle, I'm sorry if I didn't seem grateful for what you did and what you're doing now." Her gaze met his. "Thank you. I'm usually the one jumping in to help others. I guess I'm not used to a man helping me the way you have today."

Michael honestly didn't know what to say. With her running a multi-million dollar construction company, it was no doubt she was a take-charge person. He would imagine she had to put out plenty of fires and would tend to put others before herself. But how was it that a woman with a face and body like hers didn't have a man catering to her every need?

He recalled Luke's comment about her probably not being able to find a date on such short notice. Maybe work kept her too busy for a social life. Then again, it could be the way she dressed. The ultra-conservative outfit wasn't doing that curvaceous body justice.

Michael moved closer to her wanting to see if her skin was as soft as it looked. Instead of touching her cheek, the way he wanted to, he said, "I'm glad I could help, even though I did overstep on the shuttle van. Let's call us even. Since I gave you a hard time with your airplane seat, maybe offering you the window seat on the shuttle can cancel out the pet name that you've given me."

She frowned. "What pet name?"

"What? You don't even remember the name?"

She started shaking her head when realization showed on her face. "Ohhh, no. You *are* an arrogant ass. The name stays."

Michael threw his head back and laughed. "And the woman has a sense of humor. What else don't I know about you?"

"I'm glad you asked. Since we have to live under the same roof for the next few days, I have some rules." She strolled into the bedroom. Her gaze bounced around taking in everything. "This suite really is lovely."

"I agree, but that's the least Luke and CJ could do for us after the mess they just pulled."

"I know. I'm shocked my sister would do something like this and what does that say about Luke that he went along with the setup?"

"It says that he would do anything to make his woman happy." Michael would have done the same thing had he been in Luke's position.

"Yeah, I guess," Peyton said, less than enthused, making him wonder if something else was going on between her and Christina.

"So about those rules," Michael prompted. "I meant what I said downstairs. I'll be a perfect gentleman."

Their gazes met and held. Unlike anyone he had met in a long while, Peyton intrigued him. Something made him want to know the beautiful boss lady better.

"I believe you," she said. She relocated the decorative pillows from the bed to a nearby chair and then pulled back the taupe-colored comforter. She folded it and placed the cover on the foot of the bed. "Oh and I get the bed. You can take the sofa."

Michael leaned against the doorjamb, folded his arms across his chest and crossed his ankles. "I can handle that. Anything else?"

"I'm too tired to lay out the rules right now."

"Do you really think rules are necessary?"

"Rule number one. No touching," she said as if not hearing his question. She lifted her blouse over her head, and a wave of excitement shot through him. His shaft stirred. It wasn't until he saw the tank top she had on beneath the shirt that he chastised himself for acting like a high school boy peeking at the cheerleaders as they undressed.

What the hell is wrong with me?

He straightened and shoved his hands into his front pant pockets. Peyton kicked off her shoes and then laid across the bed on her stomach, her firm butt catching his attention.

Michael cursed under his breath. The last thing he needed was to be jonesing over his best friend's future sister-in-law. He promised he would be a gentleman, and he intended to keep that promise.

"Before we start setting up rules maybe we should take some time to get to know each other, especially since we have to pretend to be a couple. I'm cool with rule number one, but if we're going to make this charade look believable, that rule is going to have to be bent."

Soft snores filled the quiet space. Michael moved closer to the bed and stared down at Peyton. Apparently, she was more comfortable with him than he initially thought. At least comfortable enough to fall asleep.

He was more curious than ever to know her story. Normally when someone stoked his curiosity, he researched them or had his assistant research them, but Michael had no intention of doing that with Peyton.

Anything he found out about her he wanted to hear from her directly.

Michael brushed the back of his hand along her cheek. It was as soft as he imagined.

"What's your story?" he whispered.

Michael didn't know how long he stood over her. All he knew was that he planned to get to know this special woman.

He covered her up and left the room.

Hours later, the bedroom door eased opened.

"Well, if it isn't sleeping beauty," Michael set aside the file he was reviewing. "Did you sleep okay?"

"Yeah, like a rock." Peyton stood in the doorway. Her wrinkled clothes, tousled hair, and sleepy eyes didn't detract from how sexy she looked. "What time is it?" She yawned and stretched, her tank top lifting just enough for him to get a peek at her smooth light skin.

"A little after eight. I was going to wake you earlier. Christina called to see if we wanted to have dinner with her and Luke. When I told her you were asleep, she suggested not waking you."

Peyton sighed and pulled out one of the dining chairs before dropping down hard on it.

"Good. If they weren't getting married, I would have been back on a plane hours ago." She folded her forearms on the table and rested her chin on them, her doe-like eyes steady on him.

Michael slouched down on the sofa and propped his socked feet on the sofa table. He was going to have fun getting to know the boss lady.

"You can barely keep your head up, maybe you need more sleep."

"I'm fine." Peyton fingered one of the crystal candle holders sitting on the table. "I'm glad Christina and Luke found each other. CJ can be a little flighty at times, and I wondered if she would ever settle down with anyone."

Michael nodded. "I know what you mean. Luke has always been a loner, so I was surprised to find out last year how serious he was about Christina."

"I might be happy for them, but I'm still mad at my sister. She was just wrong in doing this to us."

"Instead of being mad, we'll have to come up with a plan to get even with them sometime during the weekend."

A smile spread across Peyton's mouth. "I can't believe I'm going to say this, but I like the way you think."

Michael laughed. "I haven't come up with an idea yet, but I'm sure together we can think of something, maybe over dinner."

"Okay, but before we do anything concerning them or dinner, we need to set some ground rules regarding our living situation."

Michael stood. He stretched his arms high over his head before letting them fall to his sides. "Yeah, you mentioned something about rules before you passed out. So let's hear them."

"Well, like I said before. No touching."

"Except for when we're in public," he added. "We have to make this couples thing look real." He chuckled at the way she narrowed her eyes at him. Oh yeah, he was going to have fun teasing Miss Prim and Proper.

"No unnecessary touching then. And when we're here in the suite, no just walking into the bedroom or the bathroom when I'm in there. Knock first."

"You act as if I have no home training."

"I don't know what you have or don't have. I don't know you, remember?"

"Well, we can remedy that. Ask me anything you want

to know."

"I plan to." She stood. "But right now I need to shower and try to wake up. It's been a long day."

He reached for her hand when she started past him.

"We're both adults on a little mini-vacation. How about we make up the rules as the need arises? In the meantime, let's just play this little adventure by ear."

"I don't play things by ear. I like to know what I'm getting into and be prepared." She pulled out of his grasp but didn't walk away.

Michael studied her for a minute. "Are you always this uptight or is something else going on?"

"I'm not uptight!" she seethed.

He lifted an eyebrow. "No? Sweetheart, you're stretched tighter than the strings on a tennis racket."

"You don't know me."

"I know what I see. I can see you're tired, but I can also see how tense you are." And he didn't think the tension swirling around her had anything to do with lack of sleep.

Peyton's shoulders sagged, and she huffed. "I'm going to take a shower." She walked away without looking back.

Michael rubbed the back of his neck and stepped out onto the balcony. So much for a relaxing mini-vacation. His beautiful roommate was already irritating the hell out of him.

Luke owed him big for this one.

Chapter Four

The next morning, Michael leaned on the railing of the balcony and stared out at the ocean. Sailboats could be seen in the distance, while surfers, parasailers, and other water enthusiasts took advantage of the perfect weather and the light breeze. He could see why people chose to retire to tropical locales. From where he stood, it was true paradise and like Peyton, he too could envision himself there on a permanent basis.

Michael had barely slept, thoughts of Peyton occupied his mind most of the night. Knowing she was nearby, behind the closed door of the bedroom, had him thinking about what ifs. What if she let her guard down and they got to know each other better? What if he kissed her and enjoyed her taste? What if...

There he went again, thinking about her in ways that would never come to fruition.

He glanced at his watch wondering what was taking her so long. He had talked her into going for a walk along the beach with him before breakfast.

The bedroom door opened. Michael glanced over his

shoulder, and his mouth went dry at the site of Peyton's backside in an aqua colored one-piece swimsuit. Her back was bare, and the sides of the suit had deep cutouts, revealing light, smooth skin. The way the garment hugged her curvaceous body and showcased her shapely legs, had Michael turning fully for a better view. His shaft shifted behind his plaid Bermuda shorts.

Hot damn.

He knew she had a smoking hot body beneath those librarian clothes, but the reality exceeded what he could have imagined.

Peyton initially held a short, matching wrap in her hand, but tied it at her waist as she glanced around the room. Then she turned to face him.

"Are you ready?" she asked, her gaze darting around, sneaking peeks at him from behind long lashes. Her behavior was so inconsistent that Michael still couldn't get a good read on her. There were moments when she came across as a badass, with witty comebacks and an I'm-not-going-to-back-down attitude. But times like this, when she could barely look at him and seemed to crawl within herself, made her come across as shy and unsure.

His gaze gobbled her up. She had her hair down. The long strands gently curled on the ends, fell around her shoulders in layers. She wore minimum makeup highlighting her expressive eyes with a light shade of eyeshadow and a touch of red on her lips. But it was the swimsuit, displaying her full, luscious breasts that had him thinking ungentlemanly-like thoughts. He already knew she had great boobs, but damn.

"Don't take this the wrong way," he started, but stopped to clear his throat, not missing the way her shoulders suddenly sagged, "but you look fine as hell in that suit."

A slow smile spread across her tempting lips, and her shoulders lowered when she exhaled. "Thank you."

Michael pushed away from the railing, walked back into the suite, and closed the slider. "So do you want to take that walk first, or grab something to eat?" He placed his hand on her back, regretting the move the moment he touched bare skin. The electric jolt that kept shooting through his body whenever he touched her was there again. By the pink tint to her cheeks, she felt it too.

"Maybe we can grab something light, walk a bit, and then come back for a full breakfast," Peyton suggested.

"Sounds good to me."

Twenty minutes later, after grabbing a quick snack, they slipped on their sunglasses and made their way to the beach. They weren't the only ones with the idea of getting in an early walk. Some couples walked hand in hand along the water's edge, while others relaxed on the loungers working on their tans, reading, or napping.

"Last night you sounded anxious about all of your family arriving tomorrow," Michael said after they'd walked a few minutes next to the ocean. Though it was hot and the sun beamed on top of their heads, the light breeze helped relieve the discomfort of the elements.

"All of them aren't coming." Peyton stopped and began removing her sandals, her feet sinking into the hot sand. Michael extended his hand, and she held on while she removed both shoes. "Thank you."

"My pleasure. You were saying?"

"Besides the resort being for couples only, no way would this place be able to handle the entire Jenkins' clan. My grandparents have seven children, sixteen grandchildren, and now great-grand kids are starting to pop up. Add spouses and extended family to those numbers and holidays and special events, like weddings, can get rowdy."

"So, it's the potential noise level that has you on edge?"

Peyton shook her head and then pushed strands of hair away from her face before glancing out at the water. She slowed her steps.

"We're a very close family. Everyone is always in each other's business."

"And what? You feel they're in your business or will be in your business?"

Peyton hesitated and started moving again. Michael kept in step wondering if she was going to answer.

"Both," she finally said. "I think they're a little worried about me. The last few months I haven't been myself."

"If not yourself, who have you been?"

She laughed, responding the way he'd hope. He had suggested the walk hoping they could get better acquainted.

"I've been a version of myself. I have a feeling that has something to do with Christina pawning me off on you like some charity case."

"Whoa. Wait!" Michael halted and stopped Peyton with a hand on her shoulder. "Where'd that come from? Because from where I'm standing, you are no one's charity case. You are a beautiful, intelligent, and witty woman. There's no way in hell there aren't men out there waiting to be the yin to your yang."

She waved him off. "Yeah, right. Trust me. Men aren't knocking down my door. It's just been a tough few years and this past year has taken its toll. I think my sister and my cousins are starting to feel sorry for me."

"Maybe they're just concerned. Two very different things. But that still doesn't answer the question about why you're anxious about them arriving tomorrow."

She turned to the water, and blew out a breath, wrapping her arms around herself. "My cousins, Toni, Jada, and Martina are like sisters to me. We all grew up together and were pretty much raised as sisters, especially Martina and I. Anyway, for the past year or two, they have all found their soul mates. Guess who hasn't?"

Michael said nothing. As a matter of fact, he was starting to think that the route this conversation was going was way outside of his expertise. He didn't do relationships, at least not anymore.

"Well, I take that back. There was a time when I thought I had found my soulmate."

"Really? So what happened?"

She turned slightly toward him. "I married him."

Shock gripped him. "Hold up. You're married?" He was going to kick Luke's ass if he had put him in a room with a married woman.

"Was married."

"Oh, I'm sorry." He ran his hand down her arm. "So what happened? If you don't mind me asking."

Again, she hesitated. Biting her bottom lip, twisting the skin gently between her teeth. "I found him and his assistant on our living room sofa."

Michael cursed under his breath, trying to come up with something to say. He could see her invisible walls going back up, and her eyes watering. She wasn't over her husband's infidelity.

Michael didn't do well with tears and did the only thing he could think to do. He pulled her into his arms and held her.

*

Peyton dropped her sandals in the sand and wrapped her arms around Michael's waist, soaking up the comfort he offered. She refused to cry over Dylan anymore. Too many tears had already been wasted on that scumbag. But she would be lying if she said that it didn't still hurt to know that she wasn't good enough for him.

"I'm sorry, sweetheart. No one deserves that," Michael whispered.

Peyton leaned back and huffed out a breath. She removed her sunglasses and hooked them on the front of her swimsuit. "I felt so stupid. I bought all of his excuses. 'Babe, I need to finish this report. Don't wait up, I'll be late for dinner. Babe, they need me in the New York office, those bozos don't have a clue. I'm still in traffic.' To this day, I wonder if there were any trips. He was probably screwing around right un—"

"Don't. Don't do this." Michael pushed his sunglasses to the top of his head. "I'm sorry I asked. More importantly, I'm sorry you went through that. I know it had to be tough."

She heard his words, but the way he was caressing her cheek and staring into her eyes, she could barely think straight. If anyone was a nice distraction from thoughts of her cheating bastard of a husband and failed marriage, it was him.

The wind picked up, and her hair blew around even more than it had been since they started walking. Sighing, she ran her hand through the loose curls. This was another reason why she usually wore it in a bun or a tight ponytail.

"I really should have put my hair up." She gathered her locks and pulled them back.

"Don't. I'm glad you wore it down." He pushed her hands away and ran his fingers through her hair. Granted the move might've been a little too intimate, but damn if it didn't feel good and sexy.

"Since I'm your better half for the next few days,"

Michael said, his voice dropping an octave. "I'm requesting that you wear your hair down whenever you're with me. I like it this way."

"Okay," she said, but she wasn't sure she'd spoken loud enough for him to hear, barely hearing herself over the pounding of her heartbeat. Heck, with the way he was looking at her and the sexiness of his voice, she would have agreed to almost anything.

Butterflies jockeyed in her belly when his hands cupped her face. His gaze slid from her mouth to her eyes and held before he zoned in on her mouth again as if contemplating his next move.

Before she could form a thought, he lowered his head, and his mouth touched hers. Her heart thrashed against her chest. The soft feel of his lips was like stepping out into the sunlight after being cloaked in darkness for years. Michael nipped at her top lip, and then the bottom one, tasting and teasing, taking her desire to a place it hadn't visited in quite a while. The phrase 'died and gone to heaven' played around in Peyton's head when he pulled her closer, deepening the kiss.

Peyton gripped the back of his shirt, pushing all thoughts of her ex and everything else out of her mind. She focused on the here and now, while Michael's experienced lips left no doubt that he knew what he was doing. She hadn't been kissed like that in years, and the sounds of the waves slapping against the rocks only increased the special moment.

Michael lifted his head, and she whimpered, reluctantly prying her eyes open. The way he searched her face, she thought for sure he was going to apologize for kissing her, and so help her if he did she was going to punch him.

"I'm too much of an arrogant ass to apologize for tasting you," he said as if reading her mind. The cocky grin spread across his mouth, sending wicked chills through her body. "Shall we continue our walk?"

Peyton cleared her throat. "Uh, yeah. Sure. That's a great idea." Before she could bend down to pick up her sandals, he handed them to her and grabbed hold of her hand.

They walked and talked as if the kiss never happened. But it was a lip-lock she wouldn't soon forget, and she wouldn't mind their tongues tangling again.

"How long were you married?" Michael asked.

"Dylan and I were married for five years."

"So the jerk's name is Dylan, huh?"

"Yep."

Peyton answered additional questions about Dylan and how she had moved on. Rarely did she talk about her ex-husband or their divorce. And for the first time, it wasn't as painful to remember.

"Are you ready to head back and get a real breakfast?" Michael asked, glancing at his watch. "Actually, it'll be more like brunch."

"That sounds good." They turned and headed back the way they came. Peyton hadn't realized they'd walked so far.

"Okay, enough about me. What's your story?" So far, her first impressions of Michael were off. He might've been cocky, but he was proving to be a nice guy. "I assume you're not married," Peyton said when he looked to be in deep thought.

"Nope. Never took the plunge and probably never will. I'm not a committed relationship type of guy."

With the patience and kindness Michael had displayed since they'd met, Peyton didn't understand his comment. They might have only been pretending to be a couple, but from what she'd seen, he would be the perfect mate for someone.

"Why not?"

"I'm just not. I've seen too much. I've done too much. And I don't think I have what it takes to make a relationship work."

"Is it because you think you would cheat?"

"No. Not all men cheat," he said simply.

"Yeah, if you say so."

"I know so." He nudged her with his arm. "My stepfather would never cheat on my mom. Luke would never cheat on Christina. There are some upstanding men out there that we both know. So don't let some jerk taint your idea of marriage. And just because it's not for me, doesn't mean you shouldn't try marriage again."

Peyton laughed. "Look at you sounding like the authority on marriage."

Michael chuckled. "Trust me. I'm not."

"Okay, so tell me more about yourself."

"There's not much to tell. I've lived in Brooklyn most of my life."

"I thought I detected a New York accent when we first met."

He laughed. "Accent, huh?"

"Yep, you definitely have an accent. So what else? Do you live in a brownstone?"

"Actually, I do. But of all the questions you could've asked me, why that one?"

Peyton shrugged. "I guess when I think of New York, I think of Times Square, Central Park, and brownstones. I've always been fascinated by some of the architectural details and character found in many of the older structures."

Michael shook his head. "I still can't believe you were an electrician construction worker. You are the *finest* electrician I've ever met."

A smile touched her lips. "Thank you." She could get used to all of his compliments. "So, tell me about the brownstone."

"I purchased it about two years ago. A real gut job that I'll probably be working on until I'm old and gray. I lived in an apartment for most of my adult life, but needed something bigger to accommodate me, and my daughter."

Peyton stopped again. "You have kids?"

He nodded. "A daughter, Michaela." His eyebrows dipped. "What's wrong?"

"Oh, nothing. I guess I'm just surprised." She started walking again. She loved children and had always wanted at least two, but she didn't date men with children.

Peyton mentally shook herself. She and Michael weren't dating. It didn't matter if he had a child. She'd do good to remember that this whole ridiculous situation was just pretend.

"So what made you become a private investigator?"

"I was a cop at first. When I decided to leave the force, a friend of mine had started a P.I. agency and asked me to come aboard." He shrugged. "I liked the work and a couple of years later, started my own business. I mainly work for defense attorneys."

"Wait. Are you the one who dug up information on Leroy Jones last year when he was trying to sue Jenkins & Sons?"

Michael nodded.

Peyton remembered Luke saying that his P.I. friend was the best in the business. Little did she know that Michael was that friend.

Shortly after moving to Cincinnati from New York, Luke had joined a law firm where he'd later been commissioned to represent Leroy, a local contractor, who was trying to sue the Jenkins family on some bogus charges. That was also the time when Christina thought Luke was conspiring against the family. All hell had broken out. Peyton hadn't thought Christina and Luke's relationship would survive the misunderstanding.

"You said that you were a cop for a few years. That's probably even more dangerous than being a P.I. What made you decide to go into that field?" She wondered if the faded scar across his neck had been a souvenir of his career choices.

Michael remained silent and kept walking. Peyton turned to see if he'd heard her question. Since he had his sunglasses on, she couldn't read his eyes, but the strong set in his jaw was a sign that the subject was touchy.

"I was a total screw up before my mother married my stepfather, Carlton, when I was nine." He shook his head as if he couldn't believe how bad he'd been back then. "Carlton was a cop and saved my ass more times than I can count. And seeing him in his uniform, looking all badass," Michael chuckled, "I wanted to be just like him."

"He must be really proud of you."

Michael hesitated before a slight smile tilted his lips. "Even after he adopted me, giving me his last name and treating me like his flesh and blood, I gave him hell. But he never gave up on me and yeah, I think he's proud. We have a great relationship now." Michael turned serious. "I don't even want to think about where I would be if he hadn't come along."

"What do you mean?" When he didn't respond, Peyton squeezed his hand. "Michael?"

"Looks like we made it back. I'm starving, what about you?"

She hesitated, not missing the way he changed the

subject, making her even more curious about him and his life.

"I guess I am a little hungry," she answered. There was more to Michael than his charming ways and great sense of humor. Maybe at some point he would feel comfortable sharing his story.

*

Tension crawled up Michael's back and settled in his shoulders as he guided Peyton to the resort. The last thing he wanted to do was talk about himself. One question would lead to another and then another, forcing him to remember years of pain, anger, and disgust. If he could, he would erase his first nine years, as well as the year Michaela was conceived. But since he couldn't, he had to live with the nightmare that was once his life.

Chapter Five

The next day, Peyton lounged on the sofa in the suite, paging through an *InStyle* magazine. She couldn't remember the last time she'd been able to peruse a magazine in the middle of the day with nothing planned.

She turned to the next page, a muscular male model with arresting eyes stared back at her, and thoughts of Michael infiltrated her mind. The time they spent together the day before had been a turning point in their relationship, or was it a friendship? Peyton wasn't sure. All she knew was that she could easily see them being friends. *Good friends.*

Flashbacks of their passionate kiss kept playing in her mind and it was hard not to imagine what it would be like if they could be more than friends.

Peyton placed her feet on the floor and leaned forward to grab a different magazine when someone knocked on the door. Before she could answer, she heard, "Open up. We know you're in there."

Peyton smiled, recognizing Toni's voice. It was safe to say the rest of the family had arrived.

She swung the door open. Her cousins Toni and Jada stood on the other side dressed like the models in the magazine she had just been looking through.

"Heyyy!" Toni said, throwing her arms around Peyton and pulling her into a hug.

"We're here." Jada blew her an air kiss as she strolled into the suite. "We thought we would come and get you to see what we can get into."

"Why are you sitting around reading?" Toni pointed at the magazines on the table and sofa. "You need to soak up as much of this sunshine and heat as you can because when we left Cincinnati this morning, it was thirty-five degrees with snow on the ground."

"That's no surprise for the end of February." Peyton reclaimed her seat on the sofa and Toni sat in the high back chair. "If you must know, I was out earlier and took a nice long walk on the beach, ate, and just got back not too long ago."

Jada picked up one of the magazines from the living room table and sifted through the pages. Rarely did she dress down like she was today, wearing a light blue satin-like sleeveless top, white shorts, and sandals with a low heel. Since hanging up her tool belt, Jada hardly ever walked around in shoes that had less than a four-inch heel. Today her outfit was simple, but probably cost a fortune. Her husband, Zack, had recently retired from the NFL and one of his favorite hobbies was to indulge his wife with expensive shopping sprees.

Jada dropped the magazine back to the table and glanced around the space. "Nice room. It looks to be the same size as ours." She walked toward the patio sliding doors and slowed, her attention on something on the floor.

Peyton followed her gaze and groaned inside.

Michael's duffel bag and a pair of brown Dockside boat shoes sat near it.

Jada pointed at the items.

"Since when did you start wearing size twelve men's shoes?"

"What?" Toni leaped out of her seat. The mother hen of the group, she always stuck her nose in everyone's business. "Why do you have a pair of men's shoes?"

Just then, the door to the suite swung open.

"Honey, I'm home," Michael announced before he walked fully into the suite. "Oh, sorry. I didn't realize we had company."

Peyton hadn't seen him for the last couple of hours, and the butterflies fluttering inside her stomach were starting to be the norm whenever he was near. After breakfast, he had walked her back to the room and left a little while later to meet up with Luke. He had also planned to go for a run. She wanted to ask what he and Luke were getting into, especially since she hadn't heard from Christina but refrained. Their pretend relationship was starting to feel a little too real.

Peyton stood, and Michael's gaze moved down the length of her body. This was the first time he had seen her in the dress she had purchased the day before from the gift shop while they were hanging out. Their undeniable connection was growing stronger by the minute.

"So what's going on here?" Toni asked. "And who are you?"

Mike extended his hand. "Michael Cutter, Peyton's...well, a friend."

Jada's brows shot up as she shook his hand. "Oh really? Why is it that we never heard of you?"

"Mike, as you probably guessed, these nosy women are

my cousins, Jada, and Toni. Or as the family refers to them, JJ and TJ."

"I figured as much. Beauty runs in the family I see, but I thought there were three of you."

"Oh yeah, Martina. She's seven months pregnant. Her husband didn't think it was a good idea for them to travel," Toni explained.

Michael nodded. "That's understandable."

He approached Peyton, his hand gripping her hip in a possessive move. Tantalizing tingles scurried up her spine, and she shivered, unable to move away despite him being sweaty from his run. If anything, she wanted to move even closer to him.

"I'm going to jump in the shower. Luke said the rehearsal dinner is at seven o'clock. Did you want to do anything before then?" The huskiness in his voice had her mind conjuring up all types of erotic things she wouldn't mind doing with him.

She shook the thought free but didn't step away from his hold. "I'm going to hang out with the girls for a couple of hours."

Peyton didn't think she would ever get used to those light-brown eyes. They glittered with mischief while his gaze bore deep into her.

"Okay," he finally said. "Well, have a nice time and I'll see you a little later." He placed a kiss against her temple and gave her hip a little squeeze as if it were the most natural thing in the world to do. "Ladies." He nodded at Jada and Toni before heading to the bedroom.

"Now that," Jada pointed to the closed bedroom door, "explains your hair, makeup, and that cute little sundress you're wearing."

Peyton glanced down at the red, black, yellow and green short dress that hooked on one shoulder and stopped above her knees. Michael had helped pick it out the day before. Hanging with him made her feel beautiful, special. It had been a long time, if ever, since she had this type of connection with a man. After Dylan, she felt undesirable, and hadn't allowed any man to get too close. Yet, being with Michael was different. It was as if they had known each other for years.

"And if this new look of yours hadn't clued us in, that expression in your eyes a minute ago says that he is either more than a friend, or you want him to be more than a friend." Toni moved closer to Peyton.

"So which is it?" Jada folded her arms.

Peyton blew out a breath. It was honestly too early to consider Michael a friend, but she'd be lying if she said that she wasn't interested in him. That thought alone seemed too crazy to voice. He still hadn't shared much about himself, and she resisted the urge to ask Christina too many questions.

"Whatever is between Mike and me is none of your business." Peyton tidied the magazines, placing them all on the table. "So are we going or what?"

They stood staring at her for a minute before Jada said, "We're going, but this conversation is not over. You have a lot of explaining to do."

"I just thought about something. If you're here with this gorgeous man, who's sending you flowers?" Toni asked.

Peyton glanced at her. "What flowers?"

"Someone sent flowers to the office yesterday. I assume it wasn't Michael since he's here with you. So if not him, then who?" Toni tapped her foot impatiently.

"You've been holding out on us haven't you?" Jada stood next to Toni with a similar scowl.

Peyton lifted her hands. "I have no idea who is

sending me flowers. Toni, I'm surprised your nosy self didn't read the card."

"MJ wouldn't let me, even shooed me out of the office."

"You're lucky we're starving otherwise we wouldn't be going anywhere until we got answers because I want to know everything. I want to know when you started seeing Michael and why we didn't know. I also want a list of who could be sending you flowers," Toni added as they headed to the door.

Before they reached the door, Peyton realized her small, across the shoulder purse was in the bedroom.

"I need to get my bag before we leave."

"Well, hurry up. I want to get out of here so you can give us details about you and Pretty-Brown-Eyes."

Peyton stilled her jittery nerves and gave a soft knock on the bedroom door before pushing it open and walking in, closing it behind her. Relief flooded through her body when she saw that the bathroom door was closed.

She hurried across the room, to the upholstered chair near the patio door where her purse lay. Ruffling through it, she confirmed her room key card was inside and then headed back across the room.

The bathroom door swung open. Steam filled the doorway before Michael stepped into view. And what an enticing view he presented. Tall, lean, and perfectly put together, he stood just inside the bedroom using a towel to dry his head and another hung low around his hips.

"Oh, hey. You're still here, huh?"

Her gaze took in the length of him, staring at his broad shoulders and wide chest that tapered down to a narrow waist. His six-pack or maybe it was an eight-pack, she wasn't sure, was on full display. No wonder he was arrogant. With a body like that, extreme perfection, he had earned the right to that huge ego. And the tattoos. Peyton had never considered tattoos sexy before, but on him…good Lord. She had seen the one on his forearm and the one on his left bicep, but the one over his heart, a decorative cross, was fascinating. She wanted to reach out and touch the elaborate design.

"Peyton?"

Her eyes shot up. "I'm leaving," she blurted, fighting to keep her attention on his eyes, but her gaze drifted to the sizable bulge behind the towel. Going lower, she took in his long, powerful legs that were on full display. Heck, he even had sexy feet.

"Okay." Amusement bounced around in his eyes. He knew he was torturing her with the sight of his tempting body. "I didn't tell you this out there, but that dress is gorgeous on you. It looks a thousand percent better than it did on the hanger."

"Thank you." Heat stormed her body. She had never blushed so much in her life. The compliments he had showered on her in the short time she'd known him, made her glad she was a woman.

Peyton glanced back at the closed bedroom door. She had to be careful. It was too easy to fall for someone like Michael – a bad-boy. He was just playing a role in Jamaica. Besides, he wasn't her type. He had a child, which meant there was a baby mama. He was arrogant like her ex-husband, and he had a dangerous job.

Nope, not her type.

"Thanks for helping me pick out the dress," she finally said, fidgeting with her purse strap.

"My pleasure."

The towel he used to dry his head, now hung around his neck as he strolled to the dresser. Apparently, he was comfortable walking in front of her half-naked. She could hear Martina's voice in her head, encouraging her to yank the towel free from around his hips.

Peyton swallowed hard. The size of his package couldn't be denied. She didn't have to remove the towel to know he was well endowed.

Michael rummaged through the dresser drawer and pulled out a pair of briefs. The night before she told him there was an empty drawer he could use. Now in hindsight, she wondered if that was a wise idea. Especially if it meant him walking around in a towel.

"So where are you ladies headed?" Michael asked, cutting into her thoughts. He gave her the perfect view of the motorcycle tattoo intricately designed across his back. And then there was his round, firm butt. *Whew*.

The naughty part of Peyton wanted to walk up behind him and palm his butt cheeks, but she had never been so bold, so brazen.

"We're going to get something to eat. But I'm not sure when we'll be back since Jada wants to do some shop—" Her words stalled in her throat when he turned and let the towel fall from his hips.

Heat crept to her cheeks, and Peyton's mouth hung open as she watched him take his time stepping into his briefs, an impressive shaft dangling between his muscular thighs. Her heart thumped wildly, her ragged breaths loud in her ears as Michael pulled the shorts up over his hips and adjusted himself.

She tried to school her features before he looked up, but warmth overpowered her body, and she had a feeling he would notice her mix of excitement and discomfort.

She wiped clammy palms down the sides of her dress, clenching her thighs together to stop the throbbing between her legs. Every nerve in her body was on high alert.

Her gaze met his. His eyebrows dipped.

Oh great, he caught her staring.

"What's wrong?" he asked as if dropping his towel, and leaving him butt naked in front of her had been no big deal.

"I...I," she muttered, unable to form a coherent thought, let alone intelligent words. He approached her, and she forced herself to stay put and not take a step back. "I'm okay."

"You don't look okay." He touched her arm, and that familiar zing shot through her body, this time igniting a fire within her. His gaze, missing nothing, studied her face. "Maybe you should sit down."

Peyton shuddered with irritation. She acted as if she had never seen a half-naked man before. Granted, never one of such perfection, but still. She was a grown, red-blooded woman acting like a doggone ten-year-old.

"Pu...put some clothes on," she stuttered. "And apparently you have forgotten my number one rule — no touching."

He stared at her for a moment and then burst out laughing. "Ahh, so that's it. You can't handle all of this male *fine*-ness" He flexed his muscles, striking erotic poses showing just how fit he was. "Oh and the no touching rule flew out the window with the kiss we shared the other day."

Peyton's frustration grew, and she clenched her teeth. She didn't know if she was more ticked at him or herself. No. She knew. Definitely herself. She let him get under her skin. Now she was paying.

"Just put some clothes on!" She pushed past him. "Arrogant ass," she grumbled on her way out the door, ignoring his laughter.

"Let's go," she snapped at Jada and Toni as she rushed

out of the bedroom, slamming the door behind her.

"Are you sure? You were in there an awfully long time. Maybe you would prefer we leave, and you stay and hang out with your boy-toy," Jada teased, strolling across the room with a wicked grin. "We don't want to block any action since it's been awhile for you."

Peyton swung the door open. "Just shut up and come on." Her cousins burst into giggles, and she rolled her eyes.

This is going to be a long day.

Chapter Six

Hours later, Michael stood at the small bar nursing a club soda, watching Peyton from across the room. The wedding party and guests were gathered in one of the small banquet rooms and had just finished the rehearsal dinner. Peyton stood talking to her parents, two of the coolest people Michael had ever met. Her mother, Violet, reminded him so much of Christina with her free-spirited attitude and easy smile. And Peyton's father, Thomas, hadn't left his wife's side, seeming to be totally enthralled with her even after almost forty years of marriage.

Michael took a sip from his drink. Despite being the only outsider, the whole family had treated him like one of their own. Although, Peyton's grandfather gave Michael pause. Steven Jenkins had slowly shaken his hand when Peyton introduced them, saying that he was surprised that Peyton had never mentioned him.

Michael and Peyton stuck to their cover story. They admitted to being introduced by Luke but didn't mention that it had only been a couple of days ago. By his behavior, the senior Jenkins was very protective of his oldest grandchild.

Michael turned back to the bar and lifted his glass to the bartender. "Can I get another?"

"If you're trying to get drunk, you're going to have to get him to add some alcohol to the drink," Luke cracked, ordering himself another beer. Michael hadn't had alcohol in years and planned to keep it that way. "So what's going on? You've been brooding all evening, and you haven't taken your eyes off of my sister-in-law since you two arrived."

"Peyton isn't your sister-in-law yet. There's still time for Christina to change her mind about marrying you."

"Ha, ha, ha, I see you got jokes. She won't be changing her mind." Luke glanced at his watch. "In less than twenty hours, she'll be my wife. I'll be the envy of every single man who knows her."

Michael chuckled. Luke was probably right. To know Christina was to love her. Hell, it might've been a family thing because her sister had his stomach all twisted up inside.

For the last few hours, he had been replaying his interaction with Peyton from when she walked in on him earlier. He didn't know why he got so much pleasure out of teasing her. Growing up with two brothers, and no sisters, Michael could only attribute his behavior to that of a guy picking on his little sister. Unfortunately, there was nothing brotherly about his feelings for Peyton. No matter how he tried shooting down the idea of there ever being anything more between them than friendship, the what ifs kept popping up in his head.

"She's getting to you isn't she?"

"Man, don't start. You know damn well that she and I wouldn't work." He wasn't the commitment kind of guy, and the last thing he would ever want to do is hurt

Peyton, especially knowing she was a little gun-shy when it came to trusting a man again.

"Don't do that," Luke said.

"Do what?"

"Act as if you're not affected by PJ. I've seen you with women. You're different around her. The way you look at her, how attentive you are, and the way you cater to her as if you two really are…" He stopped, remembering where they were. "You like her. A lot. I just hope you're not holding back because of the sins of your old man and your grandfather."

Michael shook his head. Why Luke kept trying to bring Lewis into every conversation that they'd had lately was a mystery to Michael. Then to mention his grandfather was like rubbing salt into an open wound.

"What do you want me to say, Luke?" Michael kept his voice low though the tension inside of him coiled tighter and tighter.

"Look, I initially disagreed with Christina's little match-making scheme. Now, I think it might've been a good idea. You've been avoiding serious relationships all of your adult life because of some supposed family curse."

"I'm not doing this." Michael turned to walk away, but Luke stopped him with a hand on his arm and nodded toward a door that led into the hallway.

Michael followed reluctantly, knowing he wasn't going to like this conversation and that Luke wasn't going to let the subject drop. As for the family curse, Michael didn't know if his biological father or grandfather's penchant for beating women was really a family curse, but he wasn't taking any chances.

"Mike, I wouldn't have gone along with CJ's idea if I thought you were a danger to Peyton. You're not them.

You're one of the best men I know, and I would go as far as saying I would bet my life on you. You would never hurt a woman. I know this and anyone who knows you – knows this. As for Peyton, don't rule her out. If there's a connection, see where it goes. Personally, I think you two are great together."

Peyton might've been good for him, but he doubted he was good for her. The dysfunction he had witnessed the first nine years of his life had left physical, as well as invisible scars. He had never put his hands on a woman with the intent of hurting her. Yet, he had always been afraid that there might be some genetic imbalance with the men on his father's side of the family.

"Mike, you haven't had a serious relationship since Michaela was born."

Michael whirled on Luke. "Have you forgotten the shit I went through? I almost lost everything. I…"

Luke lifted his hands. "Chill man. You know I haven't forgotten. Like you, I will never forget."

Michael took a breath and released it slowly. Of course, Luke hadn't forgotten. He had barely been out of law school when Michael called him from the hospital, under police custody. It had been one of the worst nights of his life. The same night he had vowed he would never enter a serious relationship again.

"Just because you found love, doesn't mean we're all cut out for that life," Michael said.

"You are. Look how great you are with Michaela. Whether you believe it or not, you're family-man material. Not only are you capable of loving someone, but you also deserve to have someone love you back."

Michael shook his head and laughed. "What has CJ done to you? She's ruined you, man! Did she put something in your toothpaste? That's why you're spewing all of this love shit."

Luke laughed. "She definitely did something to me because I can't imagine my life without that woman."

"And don't you forget it either," Christina said when she stepped between them. Her style of dress, from the huge hooped earrings to the long multi-colored dress with weird shapes, was so different than the way the women Luke used to date dressed.

"I was just telling my brotha here that he and Peyton would be great together," Luke explained to Christina.

"I agree. I see how you two look at each other when you think no one is watching."

Michael dropped his head. "Not you too."

"Hey, you're never going to find anyone better than my sister. She's the total package – brains, beauty, and she doesn't take crap from anyone." Christina sang her sister praises. "And I think you have the power to win her heart."

"Seducing the boss lady is not on my list of things to do. I came on vacation for some R&R, not to participate in some matchmaking scheme. Peyton is a beautiful woman. I doubt she has or will ever have any problem finding a man — on her own." He looked at Christina pointedly. "She doesn't need anyone sticking their nose in her business."

Christina waved him off. "Clearly you don't know my sister well. If my cousins or I don't intervene, she'll spend the rest of her life alone and miserable."

"And so I'm supposed to be the cure?" Michael never understood why women felt they had to get involved in each other's affairs.

He glanced at the door to the banquet room. Maybe seducing the boss lady wasn't a bad idea. They were both adults, and they were on vacation. Then again…

"I don't want to hurt her," Michael said under his breath.

"You're not going to hurt her," Christina said, punching him softly in the arm. He hadn't intended to say that out loud. "And I know this because if you do, my cousin Martina will hunt you down and kick your butt."

"Is that the carpenter?" Michael asked Luke, who was laughing and shaking his head.

"Yep and CJ isn't exaggerating. Martina is very protective of her family. Don't mess up." Luke chuckled. "We'd better get back in there since this party is for us."

Luke and Christina walked away hand in hand, and for a second, Michael entertained the thought of seducing Peyton. They had a connection, and he would be lying if he said he wasn't interested in learning more about her. However, that little doubt that always seemed to surface whenever he showed the slightest interest in a woman crept along the back of his neck. He would just as soon die before hurting Peyton.

Later that night, Michael and the guys sat around playing poker in the small banquet room where the rehearsal dinner had taken place.

"Are you sure this is the way you want to spend your last night of freedom?" Zack asked Luke.

Michael hadn't seen Zack in a couple of years, except for on television commentating football games for ESPN. They used to hang out whenever Zack wasn't playing and was in New York. Since marrying Jada, he spent most of his time with his wife.

"Yep, what better way to spend my last day of bachelorhood than with my boys?"

"I could think of a few different ways," Michael said pointedly, eliciting chuckles from Zack, Craig - Toni's husband, and Jerry, Christina and Peyton's brother.

"If you're talking about a strip club, that's probably not the best idea since we have a youngin in the group." Luke nudged Jerry.

Jerry grunted. "I'll have you know that I am plenty old enough to watch some sexy, naked woman shake what her momma gave her."

"Speaking of clubs, I heard the girls are planning on hitting up a night club a few miles from here," Luke said.

"Yes, against my better judgment," Craig grumbled. "I told Toni I didn't think them leaving the resort alone was a good idea."

Zack grunted. "I'm sure that went over well."

"Yeah, about as well as you would expect."

"Hold up, wait. You guys are letting them go to a club by themselves?" Michael asked. Peyton hadn't mentioned they were leaving the resort.

All the men in the room cast odd looks at him. "What?"

"You clearly haven't had enough experience with a Jenkins' girl." Zack shook his head.

"What the hell does that mean?"

"It means you don't tell them what they can or can't do. You just listen and respond, 'yes, dear.'" Luke chuckled. "I learned that lesson the hard way."

They all laughed at what must have been some inside joke.

"Well, I'm out of here." Michael tossed his cards on the table. "No way am I letting Peyton go to some club…" his voice trailed off when he caught what he had just said. His gaze collided with Luke's amused one.

Oh damn. Days of playing house and he sounded like a possessive asshole.

Michael dropped back down in his seat and picked up his cards. "Whose deal is it?"

The room erupted in laughter at his expense. He deserved it. He would never be able to deny that he was the jealous type, but for a moment there, he had forgotten that Peyton wasn't his.

"Tell him what happens, Craig, when you go all He-man on a Jenkins' girl," Jerry cracked, and the others chuckled.

Craig scowled, grumbling something under his breath while the others ragged him.

"So what lesson did Craig learn?" Michael wanted to know.

"A lesson we've all learned at one time or another with our women," Zack said.

Michael was more curious than ever now. Based on their behavior at the rehearsal dinner, the girls were definitely a lively bunch.

Craig shook his head, acting as if this were the last thing he wanted to talk about. "Let's just say, they do whatever the hell they want. The more you protest, the more likely they are to do something crazy."

"Like go out with a stranger, end up in a drug house, and then get arrested with their face plastered all over the television because of an unexpected drug raid," Jerry added.

"What?" Michael sat stunned. "Okay, you can't just leave me with that."

Jerry filled Michael in on the night that took place while Toni and Craig were dating. "It's a good thing Craig is a cop. Well, a police detective now," Jerry said. "Otherwise, Toni might still be behind bars."

"Man, stop. It wasn't that bad. My baby just happened to be at the wrong place at the wrong time." Craig stood and grabbed a few beers from a cooler on a nearby table. They had ordered a few bottles as well as snacks to get them through the evening.

Michael listened to one story after another from Luke, Zack, Craig, and Jerry about Christina and the other Jenkins women. When he asked whether or not Peyton ever got into trouble, they all agreed that she was the sane one of the group, the voice of reason.

"Although lately my sister has been trippin'," Jerry started while dealing the cards. "She even tried firing me a few months ago. She's been acting like a real bit—"

"Be careful, man." The words left Michael's mouth before he could stop them. A spike of irritation coursed through his veins. Peyton might have been a few things, like highly reactive, standoffish, with a smart mouth, but he wouldn't sit back and let anyone, not even her brother, disrespect her by calling her names.

"Oh, my bad." Jerry lifted his hands, palms out. "I didn't know you and my sister were like that."

"We're just friends," Michael hurried to say, kicking himself for acting like he and Peyton were more than acquaintances.

"You have to forgive my friend here, Jerry," Luke said, gripping Michael's shoulder and giving it a slight squeeze. "He's always been quick to come to the defense of a damsel in distress."

Flashbacks flared inside of Michael's head. A time when he almost lost his life, in more ways than one. Feeling Luke's hand on his shoulder reminded him of his friend's help during one of the darkest times in his life.

"You alright?" Luke shook him, and Michael shrugged Luke's hand off his shoulder.

"Yeah, yeah. I'm fine." He glanced at his cards, suddenly not in the mood for poker. At the moment, thoughts of Peyton were screwing with his mind. He dropped the cards on the table and stood. "Listen, I'm going to get some air."

He headed to the door, feeling everyone's gaze on his back.

"Mike," Luke called out, and Michael glanced over his shoulder. "If you decide to head to the club, let me know. I'll go with you."

"We'll all go with you," Craig added.

Michael chuckled and shook his head. He had a feeling they were hoping he'd go in search of Peyton. That would give them all an excuse to go and find their women without any backlash.

"I'll be in the lobby in thirty minutes." Michael strolled out of the room thinking he must be crazy going in search of a woman who had more rules than Leroy Jethro Gibbs on NCIS. Still, he looked forward to seeing her.

*

Peyton staggered off the dance floor wiping her forehead with the back of her hand. Between the heat, high-tech lights, and the club's sound system, the slight headache she'd had earlier had bloomed into a steady thump inside of her skull. But she wasn't going to complain. She needed the night out.

She moved between a few tables to get to hers. The club certainly catered to the tourists, though there were a few locals in the mix. Peyton knew now why all of the resorts were booked up. Spring break was in full effect. The majority of the crowd was under twenty-five.

"Girl, you're rockin' that dress," Jada said when Peyton made it back to their table.

"Thanks." She felt beautiful in the white, crystal embellished dress that she had picked up during Jada's mandatory shopping trip. Based on the attention Peyton was getting from the men, the dress had been a good choice even if she was overdressed compared to the college kids.

At first, she had balked at buying clothes, but Jada had been right. She insisted it was time Peyton started a new chapter in her life. A chapter that would give her permission to leave the past in the past and enjoy life again. That's exactly what she planned to do. The purchase of the short, chiffon dress, represented the start of a new chapter in the book of Peyton.

Over the last few months, she had been thinking more about finding love, getting married and having a family. No easy feat when she kept a barrier around her heart and rarely dated. Trusting again was proving to be hard thanks to Dylan. But tonight, tonight she wasn't thinking about cheating husbands, her lonely life, or Michael. The latter was easier said than done.

Peyton chugged the last of the apple martini. With her parched throat, she wanted another one.

She lifted her glass. "Need more."

"PJ, don't you think you've had enough?" Toni asked from across the table. "That's your fourth drink."

"IsitIlostcount!" Peyton's indiscernible words tumbled from her mouth. "*Gooood* I'm not drivin'." She stood, but Christina yanked her back down in her seat.

"Maybe you should sit here for a while. Between drinking and dancing, I think you can use a break."

"She's right PJ. You've had enough," Toni added. "And what the heck was that on the dance floor? That last guy was all over you."

"And I can't believe you've been able to keep the beat since you're drunk," Jada added. "God only knows how many toes you've stepped on out there."

"I'm not drunk. Tipsy maybe. Not drunk," Peyton slurred." She sipped from the water Toni placed in front of her. The cool liquid felt good going down and felt even better when she placed the glass against her forehead. "Jada, go fix their air conditioner. It's a thousand degrees in here."

Jada had been a sheet metal worker before she married Zack. Her cousin hated the dirty work, but liked the pay and was good at her job when she wasn't complaining about the work.

"You have lost your mind. Me," Jada plopped a hand on her hip, "manual labor? In this?" She pointed to her body-hugging, strapless red dress. "Yeah, right! That's not gonna happen."

"PJ, it's warm, but it's not that hot. You're probably feeling the effects of the alcohol and the crowded dance floor," Toni said and poured Peyton another glass of water from the pitcher she had requested earlier."

"So does this," Jada waved her hand up and down at Peyton, "drunken stupor have anything to do with that cutie-pie private investigator you're knocking boots with?"

"I'm not drunk," Peyton slurred again, "and the P.I. and me – friends. Just friends." The words felt bitter on her tongue and sounded gloomy to her ears. She liked Michael – a lot, but nothing could ever come of the crush, she'd develop. Soon they would be going their separate ways.

"I knew it," Christina yelled over the music, which seemed to be getting louder. "You do want to be more than friends with him don't you? Does that mean you two haven't…"

"You guys have to be the nosiest people in the world. Mind your own business, especially you." She pointed at Christina. Had she not played games with the room reservation, Peyton wouldn't be sitting there drowning her sorrows because the "cutie-pie" was treating her like his little sister. Well, maybe not his little sister. Big brothers didn't look at their sisters the way Michael had stared at her during dinner. Or the way he ogled her when he saw her in the white dress tonight. Most importantly, a big brother wouldn't have kissed her the way he had the other day.

Peyton groaned. There she was thinking about him again. She stood abruptly, regretting the quick move and grabbed hold of the chair. Okay, maybe she was a little more than tipsy. One more drink and then she would call it quits. Then again, maybe she wouldn't stop drinking until she could wipe Michael from her mind.

"I'll be back."

She ignored their protests and kept walking, staggering a little until a college kid stepped in front of her.

"Would you like to dance?" he asked, his deep voice easily rising above the loud bass filling the space.

Most of the people in the building were under twenty-five, but this guy looked to be older. Nice looking with a tall, muscular build and broad shoulders. Probably a football player.

"Sure, why not," Peyton finally responded. Maybe dancing with a hot guy would help her forget her good-looking, arrogant ass roommate.

Chapter Seven

Frustration rattled through Michael as he roamed around the nightclub. This was the second club they had stopped by and he was glad it was inside of a hotel. The last one, in a rundown building, had all of his senses on high alert when they walked in. After thoroughly checking the place, and not finding the girls, he asked around and determined there was a more popular club where many of the tourists frequented.

Michael glanced around the crowded space, barely able to hear himself think with the music blasting. Where was she and why wasn't she sticking close to the others? Toni told him that Peyton had been on the dance floor for the last fifteen minutes. In a sea of floral attire, he should have been able to spot her in that white, skimpy dress that had taunted him earlier.

"Wanna dance?"

Michael gazed down at the little girl who had pink and green hair, a nose ring, and a fitted dress that appeared three sizes too small. She didn't look old enough to go outside by herself, let alone be partying in a club.

"No thanks." He kept moving. *Women*, or in this case, little girls. He wished he would catch his daughter, Michaela, approaching a man about dancing. He would wring her neck. Granted, since she was five, he had many years before he had to worry about something like that, but it didn't sit well with him that women approached men instead of the other way around. Another thing he needed to teach his daughter.

Michael slowed. No Peyton. No way would the girls let her leave the place by herself. She had to be there still. Unease crept through his body. What if something had happened to her?

Michael stalked toward the hallway that led to the restrooms but halted in his tracks.

"What the…"

Shock stirred inside of his gut. And a burst of annoyance propelled him toward Peyton, hugged up with some guy on the edge of the dance floor. Beefy hands gripped her butt and anger plowed through Michael's body like a recently launched rocket soaring through the atmosphere.

His mind took him back to a time that he'd tried like hell to forget. A time when rage high-jacked his body, and his fists had reacted before getting his brain in gear. A time when bones cracked and blood gushed uncontrollably. A time when his whole world fell apart because he reacted before thinking.

Remembering that nightmare did nothing to slow his pace or his desire to yank the man's arms out of their sockets.

"Get off me!" Michael heard Peyton ground out as she pushed the guy back just as Michael approached from behind her. "I told you, I'm done dancing. Now go!"

Michael slowed, fists balled at his sides.

She's fine. She's fine. Relax. She's fine.

The words looped through his mind, his heart still thumping as if it would beat right out of his chest.

Peyton's dance partner's gaze met Michael's angry one, and the guy lifted his hands out in front of him. "Sorry." His terrified eyes darted from Michael to Peyton and back to Michael. "I didn't...I mean... Sorry." He quickly turned and scurried away.

Relax. She's fine. She can take care of herself.

The words continued to play inside of Michael's head.

Peyton mumbled under her breath as she smoothed down the back of her dress. She turned around and froze.

"Michael." The word came out breathy. A light sheen of perspiration covered her face and neck, but what snagged his attention were her eyes. Red. She patted her forehead with the back of her hand and then did the same to the front of her neck. She wiped her hands down her sides despite wearing a white dress. "Wh...What you doin' here?"

Before Michael opened his mouth to speak, the DJ slowed things down, playing a slower reggae song.

"Dance with me," he said and pulled Peyton toward the middle of the dance floor without giving her a chance to say yay or nay. He eased her against his body and placed a lingering kiss on her sweaty cheek before he started moving to the beat of the music. She remained silent, no protests about his forwardness or that he was touching her.

Halfway through the song, Michael winced when she stepped on his foot. When she did it again a few minutes later, he loosened his grip and leaned back, forcing her to meet his gaze.

"Sooorry," she said before he could ask if she was okay. "Your feet shouldn't be so big."

He chuckled at her slurred words. "You're drunk." He tightened his arms around her slim waist. "Just how much have you had to drink?"

"Didn't count."

The huskiness of her voice descended on him like a lover's caress, and he held her closer as they rocked to *Never Find*, a jazzy, reggae number by Jah Cure. Michael had heard the song before, but a few of the lyrics stuck out, especially the part – *I'll never hurt you*. Despite what he was starting to feel for Peyton, nothing could happen between them. It didn't matter that she had somehow pried open a portion of his heart that had been closed for as long as he could remember.

Michael nuzzled her neck, inhaling her familiar scent that was mixed with sweat. She felt good in his arms, a little too good. With each sway of her hips, his shaft throbbed, her sexy body rubbing against his. Dancing seemed like a nice idea at first, but now he wasn't sure.

Peyton seemed to move closer to him, if that were possible, their bodies practically one. Michael's hands started on her back but moved lower to grip her curvaceous hips. He knew he agreed to keep his hands to himself, but he couldn't.

Damn, she felt good.

"Glad you're here," Peyton mumbled. Her steps slowed, and she placed tiny kisses on his chest where his shirt was opened.

Their gazes met. An invisible force drew their mouths to each other. When Peyton's lips parted, Michael used that as an invitation to dive in. He tasted the liquor on her tongue as their mouths mated. Licking. Sucking. Kissing her felt natural. Perfect.

Everything faded to the background. Their tongues continued to tangle. Michael squeezed her firm ass, and a blast of desire shot straight to his shaft. No doubt she felt his erection pressed against her belly. God, he wanted her, but if he didn't put some space between them soon, she was going to feel a lot more.

Just then, she moaned, her hips moving, even more, grinding against him and Michael was a goner.

He pulled his lips from hers. "Let's get out of here."

Thirty minutes later, they were back at the suite. Michael cursed Luke and Christina for setting him up. He was a strong man, but he didn't know if he was strong enough to keep turning down Peyton's advances.

On the ride back, while kissing and groping her, he came to his senses. Not only was she drunk, but he was horny as hell. He wanted nothing more than to get her naked and bury himself deep inside of her. That couldn't happen. Peyton wasn't one-night-stand material. If they went further than kissing, she would be the one getting hurt in the end and Michael would never forgive himself.

"You walk around looking like hot sex on a stick and you're tellin' me you don't want this? You don't want me?"

Sex on a stick? What the hell?

Michael stood a few feet from the bed. He walked into the bedroom five minutes ago, after entrusting Peyton to get herself undressed. Since then, he maintained his distance like a little punk, afraid of getting too close. This was his way of keeping himself from doing what he really wanted to do – taste her again. But this time he wanted all of her, not just her mouth.

That was the problem. When he practically carried her out of the club, after telling her family they were leaving, he had every intention of having sex with her. He couldn't do it. He wouldn't take advantage of her, at least that's what he kept telling himself.

Peyton lifted the sleep shirt over her head and tossed it to the floor, her gaze steady on him as she laid back against the pillows. Full, suckable breasts hung free and Michael cursed under his breath. He'd picked a lousy ass time to be gallant.

"Are you sure you don't want this?" She slid her hands painstakingly slow over her chest, cupping and squeezing her breasts.

Michael's mouth watered, his fingers itched to touch her, and his shaft throbbed with need. "Peyton…"

She ignored him. Her eyes drifted closed and the lower part of her body, covered by the thin sheet, moved in tuned to her moans ricocheting around the room.

Lust groped through Michael's veins, shooting blood straight to his penis, but he stayed rooted in place. Who the hell was this woman? No way was she the same stiff-necked person that kicked him out of her airplane seat only days ago. Clearly, all of her damn inhibitions had been drowned out by whatever the hell she'd been drinking.

Peyton's tongue slithered out of her mouth and did a leisurely glide across her bottom lip as she teased and pinched her pert nipples.

"Shit." If her intent was to drive him insane, damn if it wasn't working.

Michael glanced away. His heart raced like a speeding bullet, charging toward its target. Hard as granite and getting harder by the minute, he took several cleansing breaths and adjusted himself, uncomfortable with the way he throbbed behind his pant zipper.

Time to put an end to this madness.

Peyton's hands were still caressing her breasts when he dropped down on the edge of the bed. Surprise flickered in her eyes as he pulled the sheet up over her tempting breasts. That was probably one of the hardest things he'd had to do in a long time. But there was something he couldn't resist.

He lowered his head and kissed her hard, unable to help himself. Liquor, mixed with her sweetness bombarded his senses, sending desire hurling through his body. He wanted her. God knows he needed her, but not now. Not like this.

With strength he didn't know he possessed, he pulled away. Still breathing hard, he stared down into Peyton's sleepy eyes and sighed.

"I have too much respect for you to have a one-night stand," he said after several long seconds.

"Your respect is not what I need right now," she countered.

For a person who'd had too much to drink, she was certainly thinking clearly...or maybe she wasn't. He hadn't known her long, but he knew enough to know that if they went through with this, she would regret it in the morning. That's not how he wanted to be remembered.

"Will you at least sleep with me? Just sleep." She patted the bed next to her.

"Boss Lady, you're killing me." Even the strongest man had his weaknesses, and she was quickly becoming one of his.

"Just for a little while. Until I fall asleep."

He groaned and stood, walking around to the other side of bed. He kicked off his shoes and started to climb in, but she stopped him.

"Lose the clothes."

His brows dipped, and he stared at her. "Exactly how many drinks did you have? Because I remember a time when I've had three or four drinks and could barely remember my name. Yet you—"

"I'm different. You said so yourself." She lay on her side, snuggling more into her pillow. She would be asleep within minutes. "Come on, Mike. We'll just sleep. I promise I won't try anything."

Michael shook his head and laughed. She said the words with a straight face, which only made the whole situation funnier. He could remember using the same line a time or two himself.

He picked up her sleep shirt and handed it to her. "Put that on." She stared at the garment without moving. "Put it on or no deal." There was no way he could lay next to her with her breasts on full display without touching them. One touch would lead to so much more.

Once she had the shirt on, Michael stripped down to his boxer briefs and climbed in under the cover. She moved closer to him, her hands in a prayer-like position under her cheek.

Unable to resist touching her, Michael pushed a lock of hair that was starting to curl, behind her ear. Sweetness. That's what he thought of as the back of his hand glided down her smooth cheek, reveling in her silky skin. She closed her eyes and released a soft sigh. Minutes later, a whisper of a snore could be heard.

Michael studied her serene face, her natural beauty shining through. How her idiot of an ex-husband could have someone as sweet as her, and then turn around and cheat was a mystery to him. Peyton was special. Michael figured that out in only a few days. If he ever decided to try a serious relationship with a woman, he'd want it to be with someone like her.

Michael moved his hand away, turned and clicked off the lamp. Moonlight shone through the bedroom's screened patio door as he stared up at the ceiling. Waves crashed around outside, the sound soothing his tired body. Maybe now he could finally get some sleep.

Awhile later, Peyton groaned next to him, and he turned just as she clutched her stomach and groaned again.

Oh no.

He shot up. "Peyton? Peyton." He shook her fully awake, thinking she was about to be sick.

"I don't feel good," she whined, pain distorting her features. She gagged, and her hand flew to her mouth.

Without a word, Michael practically dragged her to the bathroom. The moment he positioned her near the toilet, she heaved, gripping the toilet bowl.

"That was close." He turned to the sink while she emptied the contents of her stomach, groaning with every gag. Wetting a washcloth, Michael glanced over his shoulder when he no longer heard her. "Feeling better?" He flushed and stooped in front of where she sat on the floor, her back against the wall.

"No."

He smiled and wiped her face and mouth.

"You might feel worse before you feel better," he said rinsing the towel in the sink before sitting on the floor next to her. He handed her the towel, and she wiped her hands.

Her sleep shirt rode up her thigh, and Michael's gaze took in her smooth legs. Wicked thoughts shot through his mind.

Michael shook his head, chastising himself for thinking how much he wanted to feel those legs wrapped around him. He dropped his head back against the cool tile and closed his eyes.

"Is this why you don't drink?" Peyton's quiet voice infiltrated Michael's thoughts. He had admitted to her that first night in Jamaica, when they'd had dinner together, that he didn't drink.

He opened his eyes. "Part of the reason." He had gotten himself into so much shit the last time he had a drink. He vowed then - never again. "My biological father was an alcoholic," he added as another reason he stopped drinking. Growing up, he knew alcohol contributed to some of his father's issues. That didn't stop Michael from having his first drink at sixteen. He wasn't an alcoholic, but he knew first hand that drinking too much could easily alter one's judgment.

"Are you ready to get back in bed?"

"I think so, but I need to rinse my mouth." Peyton stood on wobbly legs, using the wall to help keep her steady.

Michael tossed the towel onto the granite vanity and wrapped his arm loosely around her waist. He helped her to the counter, pouring some mouthwash in one of the paper cups.

When she finished freshening up, she released a long drawn out sigh but didn't move.

"Are you done?" He nudged her when it looked as if she had fallen asleep standing.

"Yes." She still didn't move.

"Here, let me help you." This all felt a little too real, Michael thought as he carried Peyton back to bed and climbed in next to her. He pulled her into his arms and kissed her forehead. "Get some sleep."

Drifting off to sleep, he imagined what it would be like to hold her every night, in his bed.

Chapter Eight

The next morning, Peyton flopped onto her back and slowly opened her eyes. She ran her tongue around in her mouth, trying to break up the feel of cotton. What had she been thinking drinking so much the night before?

Never again, she thought as she turned onto her side. Her brows shot up, and she gasped when her gaze slammed into Michael's. Memories of the night before bombarded her mind all at once, and she groaned in embarrassment.

"Good morning." His deep, sleep-filled voice tugged at her heart-strings.

"Morning," she mumbled. Swallowing her pride, she said, "I'm sorry about last night. I—"

"You have nothing to be sorry about." He touched her cheek but quickly pulled his hand away. "How do you feel?"

"Like I had too much to drink. My head feels as if a hippopotamus is sitting on it."

Michael chuckled. "Can't say I ever heard it put that way before." He reached behind him and turned back around with an oversized shot glass filled with green liquid. "Drink this."

Peyton leaned away from him. "I'm not drinking that…whatever it is."

"It's pickle juice, egg whites, and peach fuzz."

"What?"

He chuckled. "I'm kidding. It's just pickle juice. It'll replenish your electrolytes and get your body back in balance. Add this with a little more sleep, and you'll feel better. I promise."

Peyton hesitated, but eventually took the glass from him. "So you just happened to have pickle juice laying around?"

"I had someone bring it up."

She sniffed before taking a small sip. Realizing the concoction didn't taste as bad as she expected, she finished the drink.

"Did you get any sleep?" She handed him the glass and laid back down, feeling as if she could sleep for a week.

"A little."

They lay on their sides staring at each other as she recalled some of the things she'd said and did the night before. She had never been so brazen and hoped he didn't think less of her.

"Thank you for last night," she said and smiled when he lifted an eyebrow at her. She realized after the words left her mouth how they must sound.

"You do know we didn't do anything, right?" Michael asked.

"I know. That's what I'm thanking you for. Though I did want something to happen between us last night, it's probably good we didn't do anything."

Peyton scratched her head and pushed hair away from

her face, imagining how bad it probably looked, but too lazy to get up and comb it.

She hadn't been thinking straight the night before. No, that's not true. She knew what she'd asked for, but hadn't thought the situation through. Yes, she wanted Michael more than she had wanted any man in a long time, but she wanted more than one night.

"So why did you want something to happen between us? Don't you remember your rules? Rule number one, no touching."

"I remember my rules. But...but my body didn't give a damn about the rules. It's...it's been awhile for me." She hadn't planned to add that last part, but it was true. She hadn't been with a man since her husband and even when they were still together, toward the end, their sex life had been almost non-existent.

"Well, for the record, I wanted you. *I want* you like a hungry man wants food, and it has been hard as hell to keep my hands off of you."

Peyton glanced at him. A thrill scurried through her body, bringing a smile to her face. In the last few days, Michael had made her feel desirable, and they hadn't done much. A small touch here and there, and then there were the kisses. Each kiss brought her body more to life.

"Well, for the record, you've done a lousy job at sticking to rule number one."

Michael burst out laughing. "You're too much." He turned onto his back, lifted his arms, moaning as he stretched his long muscular limbs up and out before dropping his arms back onto the bed. "Regardless of how things started out between us, I think I'm going to miss you."

Peyton punched him in the arm, laughing. "You better. 'Cause I'm going to miss you too." She had given him a hard time initially, but tomorrow they would go their separate ways. Peyton didn't know if she would ever see him again once they left Jamaica, but she would never forget the way he made her feel.

Hours later, Peyton, Michael, Luke and the wedding officiant stood under a white gazebo, the ocean as their backdrop. The setting sun cast a romantic ambiance over the already peaceful evening. Now Peyton understood why Christina wanted to get married in Jamaica. It truly was paradise.

Peyton's gaze met Michael's. He had been watching her since she arrived on the beach. She swallowed, trying not to fidget under his intense stare. Her body pulsed when he looked at her like he wanted to rip her clothes off and make wild, passionate love to her. She had seen the expression often over the last four days – in her swimsuit, after the kiss on the beach, in her new clothes, at the rehearsal dinner, and again when they returned from the club. Each time his gaze intensified.

When Eric Benet's, *Spend My Life With You* began playing, Peyton diverted her attention to where Christina and their father stood. Thomas Jenkins was handsome in his white tuxedo, less the jacket, as was the case with Luke and Michael. But it was Christina who garnered all of the attention. The long, white, crochet hippie-like wedding gown with bell sleeves was gorgeous and looked as if it was made specifically for her. When in fact, Jada had found the dress on one of her many shopping ventures.

The family members sat in folding chairs facing the gazebo. Everyone stood and turned as Christina and their father walked the short distance.

Peyton's gaze collided with Michael's again. The song's lyrics taunted her, making her imagine how the words would sound coming from Michael as he whispered them in her ear someday. That just maybe he was feeling for her, what she felt for him.

"Family and friends, we are gathered here today…"

The officiator's words cut into Peyton's thoughts, shaking her out of her ridiculous fantasy. Michael had made it clear that morning that he only saw her as a friend, a friend he wouldn't mind having sex with. He claimed he wasn't a long-term relationship kind of guy. Peyton disagreed. He was absolutely relationship material.

*

No matter how much he tried, Michael couldn't take his gaze off of Peyton. He knew Christina and Luke should be the center of attention, but his eyes wouldn't cooperate. It was as if Peyton had put a spell on him, forcing all of his attention on her. It didn't help that she looked like a goddess in the short, strapless peach dress that hugged every luscious curve of her body. All he could think about was stripping her out of it to get another glimpse at what lay beneath the silky garment.

Peyton fiddled with the bouquet of flowers in her hand. He knew he was making her uncomfortable, but Michael didn't glance away. He still enjoyed messing with her even if they weren't verbally sparring.

Earlier over breakfast, she had questioned him about his dating status. He knew what she was fishing for, the same thing he had been thinking about – staying in touch to see if what was happening between them could turn into something more. Michael knew himself well enough to know he couldn't give her what she wanted.

"Ladies and gentlemen, I present to you, Mr. and Mrs. Lucas Hayden" the officiator announced.

Cheers and whistles went up all around as the couple kissed. When Luke and Christina finally came up for air,

Luke turned to Michael.

"Well, I did it. I'm a married man." Luke beamed.

"I can't believe you went through with this," Michael teased hugging his friend, truly happy for him. "I guess it's up to me to keep the bachelor's life alive."

"For now. I have a feeling your day is coming sooner than you think." Luke pounded Michael's back before they released each other.

"I don't know who you've been talking to, but someone is feeding you wrong information, my friend. I'm never getting married."

Chapter Nine

"You're fired!" Peyton slammed the file cabinet drawer and turned to her brother. "I've had enough. You can't just go into these client's homes or place of business and do whatever you want. When I give you a work order, there are specific details of what you're supposed to do."

"PJ, the client liked the light fixture that I picked out. I don't know why you're making such a big deal about this."

Her body trembled, barely holding her anger in check. "I'm making a big deal about this because you keep doing the same damn thing. Screwing up a job over and over is not how Jenkins & Sons operates!"

"You know what? I thought the trip to Jamaica would mellow you out, but instead, you came back even bitchier than before. I don't know what your problem is, but deal with it and leave the rest of us the hell alone!"

Peyton's body jerked in surprise, hurt strangling her vocal cords. Jerry had never talked to her like that before. She knew she'd been hard on him, but firing him wasn't an emotional response.

Drawing deep within herself, she steadied her breathing and sat behind her desk. "Get out," she said calmly, despite the impatience raging through her. "And leave your ID and keys with Tammy. Your last check will be mailed to you."

"I'm not leaving because I'm not fired." He leaned on the desk facing her. "The day you left for Jamaica, MJ told me I was doing a good job. So I'm not—"

Peyton lunged out of her chair. "I want you out of my office. Now!"

"That's enough!"

Peyton and Jerry jerked their heads toward the entrance where Steven Jenkins filled the doorway.

"I can hear you two all the way down the hall." Their grandfather stepped in, and slammed the door.

"Pops, she's trying to fire me. Isn't there a process or warnings employees are supposed to get before being fired?"

"I've given you plenty of warnings!"

"Not written ones!" Jerry shouted.

"Okay, that's enough. Jay, leave your sister and me alone for a minute." Her grandfather sat in one of the guest chairs in front of Peyton's desk and she already knew she was about to get one of his famous lectures.

"Sis, I'm sorry. I didn't mean some of the things I said." Jerry turned to leave but stopped. "Actually, I take that back. I meant what I said. I just could have said it differently." He cocked that crooked smile that used to get him anything he wanted from her when he was little.

"Oh shut up and get out of my office," she said, some of the anger lifted from her voice as she reclaimed her seat. He always got on her nerves like most kid brothers, but she still loved him.

"So how many times have you fired Jerry?" her grandfather asked, humor in his voice.

Peyton rubbed her forehead, frustration jockeying inside of her chest. She had "fired" Jerry at least five times in the past year, but never followed through. Eleven years apart, she and Jerry had a good relationship, for the most part. She might've spoiled him when they were growing up, but now Peyton needed him to behave like an adult and take responsibility for his mistakes. His good looks and charming personality were only going to take him so far.

"Care to tell me what's really going on?" Steven asked as he crossed his legs and folded his hands on his lap.

Peyton sucked in a deep breath and released it slowly. "Grampa, he's been screwing up jobs. Then he turns around and suggests either a different service or product to the client and they let his screw up slide."

Steven Jenkins cocked an eyebrow. "So in the end the client is happy, and the job is done?"

Peyton lowered her gaze. "Yes." So what's the big deal? Why was she constantly on Jerry's case? Why had she fired him, again? Those were the questions she expected from her grandfather, but they never came.

"In Jamaica, you seemed happier than I've seen you in a long time. I assume it had something to do with the young man you were with."

Since returning home, not a day went by that Peyton didn't think of Michael, wondering how he was doing. Despite knowing that what they had shared was temporary, she had fallen for his arrogant ass.

"Jamaica was a great trip. It felt good to get away." It also felt good to pretend she was someone else for a while without all the responsibilities and memories of past hurts.

Peyton's shoulders slumped with the realization that she couldn't run away from her problems. They were still here, still buried deep inside of her.

Tears pricked her eyes, and she blinked several times to keep them at bay. If she were honest with herself, she was better off before going out of town. At least then, she hadn't known what she'd been missing. Spending time with Michael, she had forgotten what it was like to have a man's full attention.

Her grandfather stood and walked around the desk. Pulling Peyton into a standing position, he wrapped his arms around her. Tears she had managed to hold at bay for the past week, spilled down her cheeks. The disappointment of returning to Cincinnati the same way she left and the loneliness of the week had finally caught up with her.

The more she thought about her lonely life, the faster the tears fell. She had no clue how to pull herself from the rut she'd dug herself into, but she had to figure it out. She couldn't keep going like this, driving herself and everyone around her crazy.

"It's okay, sweetheart. Everything is going to be fine." Her grandfather rubbed her back.

Peyton accepted the Kleenex he stuffed into her hand and quickly wiped her face. "Sorry." She stepped out of his arms and sat on the edge of the desk.

"I know I don't say this often enough, but I love you. I'm proud of all that you have accomplished. You stepped into the lead role here when no one else was willing and you've taken this company further than I thought possible. But PJ, this place cannot be your whole life."

"Grampa—"

"You need a break. That spark I usually see in your

eyes is gone. I couldn't remember the last time I saw it until we were in Jamaica and you were dancing at the wedding with Michael."

Peyton hadn't realized her grandfather had paid her any attention while on the trip. It wasn't like they spent much time in the same space. As for Michael, he made her laugh and forget her troubles. And sure he had stirred a desire within her that had her ready to drop her panties, but—

"That's the look right there."

Peyton glanced at her grandfather, who was smiling. Heat rose to her cheeks at the route her thoughts had taken, but she said nothing.

"This company has been your whole life, and that's not the life I want for you. When I was running the business, your grandmother was the one who made sure I kept a good balance." He chuckled. "She once told me that there was no way she was coming second to Jenkins & Sons Construction. Trust me, over the years, there were plenty of times she had to remind me that this was just a job, not my life. So now I'm reminding you. It's time for you to use some of those vacation days that you have accumulated."

Peyton smiled. Everyone knew Katherine Jenkins was in charge of the Jenkins family. Sure their grandfather made the tough decisions, gave the great lectures, and in most cases was the go-to person in the time of need. Her grandmother was the glue that kept the family together.

"I don't know if it's a good time to be away from the office. I just submitted bids for several big projects and—"

"And this company is not going to fall apart without you, PJ." He kissed the top of her head. "You need some time off. Travel or take up a new hobby. Whatever it takes to get your joy back, do it."

Peyton didn't have a clue on how to reclaim her joy. She wasn't even sure when she'd lost it. As for traveling and learning a new hobby, working long hours didn't allow much time for thinking about hobbies or a social life.

"Take at least a month off. Longer if you need to."

"A month, Grampa? Who's going to take care of everything around here?"

"Martina and Nick did a great job while we were in Jamaica. I'm sure they can handle a month."

"MJ goes on maternity leave soon, and there's too much work for Nick to handle by himself." Granted Peyton did a big chunk of the work herself, but after so many years she had learned to multi-task and prioritize.

Her grandfather gripped her shoulders. "Peyton, you're going to take some time off, and we'll take care of the company."

"But I haven't had time to prepare them or get anything in order."

"Okay, your leave starts Monday. That gives you five days to transition the work to the team."

The office door swung open, and Martina waddled in carrying a large bouquet of yellow roses.

"Oh, hey, Grampa. I didn't know you were still here," she said, handing Peyton the flowers. "Special delivery."

"For me?" Peyton asked, remembering the flowers her ex-husband had sent while she was in Jamaica.

"Okay, girls. I'm heading out. Peyton, remember what I said. Oh, and if you're receiving flowers, that means you have someone who can help take your mind off of work."

Peyton smiled and shook her head. "Bye, Grampa."

"What was that all about?" Martina asked, plucking the card from the flowers. Peyton snatched it from her.

"Grampa wants me to take some time off," Peyton said absently, as she scanned the card.

Just thinking about you. Hope all is well. Dylan.

"Okay, first who are the roses from? And second, I agree with Grampa." Martina grabbed the card from Peyton's hand. "Dylan? What the heck, PJ? Why is he suddenly sending you flowers? That's twice in a couple of weeks."

"Hey, your guess is as good as mine."

"Please tell me you haven't given that jerk any reason to think you would give him another chance."

"I haven't spoken to Dylan since our divorce was final and I plan to keep it that way." Peyton carefully removed the flowers from the glass vase and tossed them in the trashcan next to her desk. "The vase is too pretty to throw out."

"Just because you toss the flowers doesn't mean he's going to go away." Martina stood next to the desk rubbing her round belly. At seven months, she wasn't very big and looked as though she had a basketball under her shirt. "I don't like it. He's up to something."

"MJ, I told you I haven't been in contact with him. I don't know why he sent the roses, and I don't care. He's still the lowest form of human life as far as I'm concerned."

Martina studied Peyton. "Good. His cheating ass lost all rights to you when he decided to screw around."

"Don't remind me."

Martina sat, sinking low in the leather guest chair. "It burns me up inside that he thinks he can send flowers and make things right between you two. And why the hell is he sending them three years later?"

Peyton wondered the same thing as she sat in her desk chair.

"When the roses arrived, I was secretly hoping they were from your boy-toy, Michael," Martina admitted. "Have you heard from him?"

"No and he wasn't my boy-toy," Peyton said for what felt like the thousandth time. She hadn't heard from Michael, and it frustrated her that she couldn't stop thinking about him. "Can we talk about something else?"

"Sure. So Grampa wants you to take some time off. What, he tryin' to help you get your groove back?"

Peyton laughed. Martina was the loud mouth in the family and had no filter. The family thought that after she married a former U.S. Senator, Paul, that she would tone down. That didn't happen, but Martina seemed happier than Peyton had ever seen her. A wonderful husband and a baby on the way, what more could a person ask for?

Don't go there.

Peyton sighed and rubbed her temples. That was part of her problem. She wanted what her cousins and her sister had found – happiness with a special man.

"Hellooo." Martina waved her hands in Peyton's face. "You were going to tell me about the time off Grampa wants you to take."

"Oh, yeah. He said I need to take some time and find my joy."

"I agree. You're driving everyone around here nuts. We can handle the office work."

"Grampa suggested a month."

"A month! Dang, that's a long time."

"I know. You guys need me."

Martina nodded. "Maybe we do, but we want the old Peyton back. The one who bossed us around with sternness, but compassion."

Peyton chuckled. "Hearing you say the word compassion is funny. What do you know about compassion?"

"I know that I don't have much of it, and you're starting to act more like me every day. I don't like it."

Peyton laughed again realizing she hadn't laughed since leaving Jamaica and Michael.

Sighing she mentally slapped herself. There she went again thinking about him. Maybe a month off would do her some good. She could regroup and maybe even find a boy-toy.

*

Three days into her mandatory leave and Peyton was about to go crazy. She plopped down on her sofa with a pint of Graeter's Bourbon Pecan Chocolate Chip ice cream and picked up the television remote. This daily routine, of eating the dessert, would have to come to an end if she planned to fit any of her clothes. She needed to find something to get into and soon.

Her cell phone rang, and she leaned forward and swiped it from the sofa table. She glanced at the screen, not recognizing the number, and debated on whether to answer. "Oh what the heck."

"Hello."

"Hello, Peyton." The baritone voice of her ex-husband caught her by surprise. "How are you?"

"What do you want, Dylan?" He was the last person she expected or wanted to hear from.

He chuckled. "Is that any way to greet your first love, the man you vowed to spend the rest of your life with?"

"You have sixty seconds to state your reason for calling. As for being my first love, you weren't," she lied. "Oh, and that vow, biggest mistake I've ever made."

Silence. For a minute she thought he had hung up until she heard traffic in the background.

"I called to see if you received the flowers. You've

been on my mind, and I just wanted you to know that I've been thinking about you. I'm sorry for the way things ended with—"

"It's been three years, Dylan. Why now? Wait, you know what? It doesn't matter. I don't care. Goodbye." She disconnected the call and dropped the phone on the sofa next to her.

In the past three years, she'd only talked to her ex twice and each time was because he wanted or needed something. The first time, he had inquired about his high school letterman jacket, which she had given to Goodwill. The last time, he'd had the nerve to ask if she could do some electrical work for him. Each time he acted as if they were friends. Like he had forgotten the crap he had put her through.

When her cell rang again, she snatched it up prepared to tell Dylan off, but it wasn't him. A sweet thrill skittered up her back seeing Michael's name on the screen. They had exchanged numbers before leaving Jamaica, but at the time, she hadn't believed he would call.

"Hello." She set her ice cream on the table.

"Hey, Boss Lady. How you doin'?" His familiar voice brought a smile to her face.

"I'm fine. So let me guess, CJ called you."

"Noo, I haven't heard from her or Luke. Why? What's going on?"

Peyton hesitated. Could it be he had been thinking about her as much as she'd been thinking about him?

A shot of adrenaline burst through her veins and like a little kid, she did a happy dance in her seat, swinging her arms and legs back and forth. She shouldn't read too much into the phone call, but she couldn't help herself.

"I'm on a mandatory leave of absence. I thought maybe CJ had mentioned it to you."

"Why? Are you hurt?" The worry in his voice didn't go unnoticed, enhancing the flutter in her stomach.

"I'm fine. According to my grandfather, and every other member of my family, I need a vacation. A long vacation. Hence, the mandatory leave. But I think I'm going to go crazy laying around the house."

"Then don't. Come..." His voice trailed off but then he continued. "While you're deciding what to do with yourself, consider coming to New York. I'd be glad to show you around and...and maybe treat you to a dirty water dog."

Peyton laughed. "A dirty water dog? Umm, I think that's something I can do without. I'm not really a dog person."

Michael's deep laughter flowed through the phone line. He explained the dirty water dog he was referring to was a New York hot dog purchased from a street vendor.

Peyton grabbed the pint of ice cream and curled back up on the sofa. She and Michael laughed, and talked like old friends, the easy conversation brought back memories of their time in Jamaica.

This is what she missed living alone. Discussing her day, laughing and feeling as if someone cared enough to listen to what she had to say. That's what Michael gave her. Back in Jamaica, when he said they could be friends, Peyton had been a little disappointed because she thought it was just a line, but now, she had a glimmer of hope. Maybe, just maybe, they could be more than friends.

Chapter Ten

Michael set his cell phone on the desk and rocked in his chair. Peyton would be in New York in five days, and he wasn't sure how he felt about that. When he invited her to visit, the words were out of his mouth before he had a chance to pull them back. But he'd be lying if he said he didn't want to see her.

Michael picked up the television remote and pointed it at the flat screen on the wall across from his desk, and unmuted the NBA basketball game. New York was down by twenty points with three minutes to go. It was safe to say they weren't going to make the playoffs again this year.

A sound near the door caught his attention.

"Daddy, can I have some water?" his daughter, Michaela, asked in that tiny voice that tugged at his heartstrings. Normally Michael heard her the moment she came out of her bedroom, but not tonight. So distracted by thoughts of Peyton, he hadn't even heard the third step from the bottom that groaned when stepped on.

"Aren't you supposed to be asleep?"

She ran over to him, her messy ponytails swinging on each side of her head. His little girl meant the world to him, and she was definitely his greatest accomplishment.

Michaela climbed onto his lap, kissed his cheek, and snuggled close knowing he couldn't resist when she nestled against him.

"You should have been asleep an hour ago."

"I was thirsty, but I'm not thirsty anymore. I wanted to give you a hug."

"Oh really?" Michael chuckled and tweaked her nose. "I think this is you stalling again. I'm starting to see a pattern. We go through this every night. Especially school nights."

Michaela lifted her head. "Was that your girlfriend on the phone?"

Michael frowned and leaned back. "What are you talking about?" This was the first time he'd spoken to Peyton since returning from Jamaica, and he hadn't mentioned her to anyone.

"Uncle Shon said he wishes you would get with your girlfriend and stop growling."

Michael fought to keep his smile at bay. Michaela was at the age where she caught everything that was said, whether it was spoken to her or not.

"So when did Uncle Rashon say this?"

The day before, Michael's youngest brother had complained about him playing basketball like a madman, claiming he probably needed to get laid. He just hoped his brother had sense enough not to say anything like that around Michaela.

"Um, when he was talking to Nana," Michaela said of Michael's mother. "He said some *things* are wrong with you. Is something wrong with you, daddy?"

Michael laughed, unable to hold back at how serious

his daughter's expression was. "No, baby, nothing's wrong with me. But what did I tell you about listening in on other people's conversations?" At five years old, not only was she book smart, but she seemed to know something about everything.

"You said to stay out of grown folk's business," she mumbled and batted long curly eyelashes at him. Eyes so similar to his stared back at him, and Michael's chest tightened with the love he felt for his little girl. Octavia, Michaela's mother, was right. Michaela did have him wrapped around her finger.

Instead of chastising Michaela more, Michael smothered her sweet face and neck with kisses, sending her into a fit of giggles.

"Daaaaddy!" she screamed, laughing and squirming in his arms. "Stooop."

"I'm not stopping until you promise to stay out of grown folk's business." He continued kissing her, adding tickling to the playful torture.

"Oookay. I pro…promise," she said trying to get away, but he maintained his hold on her.

Once they settled down, Michaela played with the buttons on his shirt. "Was that your girlfriend you were talking to?" she asked again.

Michael shook his head. "What am I going to do with you, kid?" He tweaked her nose, causing more giggles from her. "I was talking to my friend."

Referring to Peyton as just a friend didn't seem like a strong enough title. Anyone who throttled his peace of mind the way she had over the last ten days, deserved a different title. It seemed he couldn't do anything without thinking about her or wondering what she was doing.

"Is she a girl?"

"Yes, Michaela, she's…" Michael started but stopped.

"I thought you wanted water."

"I changed my mind."

"Well, then you can go back to bed."

She dropped her head to his chest and wrapped her little arms around his waist, mumbling something about wanting to stay with him. Instead of making her go back to bed, he kissed the top of her head and held her close while he caught the end of the basketball game.

Michael never thought he had the capacity to love someone as much as he loved Michaela.

When Michael and Octavia started hanging out, he hadn't intended for their union to produce a child. It wasn't until the day he had planned to break up with her did she tell him she was pregnant. That night changed his life in many ways, some good, some bad, but his daughter had definitely been the good.

Michaela's soft snores brought him back to the present. He stood and headed for the stairs. Yep, this was starting to be a pattern with them, but there was nothing he would change about the bedtime ritual. When Michaela had turned two, Octavia landed the job of her dreams, which involved traveling three out of four weeks a month. She had signed over full custody to him. At first, the idea of caring for a toddler 24/7 scared the hell out of Michael. But thanks to his family, the adjustments went smooth over the years and they had settled into a good routine.

Michael laid Michaela on the twin-sized bed and covered her with the pink and white comforter. Sitting on the edge of the bed, he took in her baby soft skin, long lashes, and pert mouth. She was definitely a beauty. Smart as a whip and such a loving child. Despite the dysfunction he had grown up with, he vowed to do everything in his power to make sure she had a normal childhood.

Michael sauntered to the door but turned back before closing it behind him. Every now and then, like now, he thought about having more children, but that would mean being in a committed relationship.

Peyton's sweet face flashed across his mind as he quietly left the room and headed back down the stairs. She was the marrying type and everything he could ever want in a woman.

Slow your roll, Mike. For all he knew, the connection he and Peyton experienced in Jamaica might be non-existent now that they were back to reality.

*

Damn. Was the only word to come to mind when Peyton swung open the door of her hotel room five days later. Michael stared into eyes that visited him every night in his dreams and a fist gripped his heart and squeezed. Nothing had changed. He still felt that same mesmeric pull, that powerful force that connected them.

His gaze went lower, taking in the low-cut, white shirt tied at her left side, emphasizing her narrow waist. Her legs were encased in a pair of black, skinny pants and black high-heeled boots were on her feet.

"Wow," he finally said when she fidgeted under his perusal. No other words were spoken. Instead, he stepped across the threshold and pulled her into his arms, devouring her mouth in a heated kiss. Lips he had dreamed of kissing again were as soft as he remembered and she still fit perfectly in his arms. The woman had control over him that he couldn't explain, and he wasn't sure if he wanted to figure it out. All he wanted was her.

Peyton gripped his shirt as if holding on for dear life, their kiss stoking the fire burning inside of him. His tongue slid in and out of her mouth, mating with hers as if they kissed all the time. God, he missed her. He didn't want to let her go, but with a strength he didn't know he possessed, he lifted his head.

Michael's forehead touched hers. "Hi." The huskiness in his voice sounded foreign even to him. He nuzzled her neck unable to help himself as he breathed in her intoxicating scent.

"Hi," she said with a little laugh, her smile squeezing his heart more. "Now that's what I call a welcome."

"I'm glad you're here."

"Me too." She kissed him again. "I couldn't wait to see you."

"The feeling's mutual." His hand rested on the side of her neck, his thumb caressing her cheek. Michael couldn't stop looking at her or touching her. It was hard to believe she was there. "Let's go and get something to eat." Because if he stayed in her room much longer, they would never leave.

As he led her out of the hotel, Michael knew he had to be careful with Peyton. He wanted her more than anything, but he didn't want to hurt her. If…when they came together, he had to make sure he was ready to give her what she wanted from a man – a commitment.

*

Hours later, Peyton and Michael stepped outside of B.B. King's Blues Club in Times Square, and a cold breeze shot through Peyton, forcing her to snuggle deeper into her lightweight leather jacket. She would have to remember to wear the heavier coat she traveled with when she ventured out the next day. It was proving to be a cold March though she thought it would be warmer on the east coast.

Michael grabbed her hand and maneuvered around a group of people waiting in line for the next show. Peyton held on tight as he shouldered his way forward.

"It's after ten p.m. I can't believe all these people are out and about," Peyton said, jogging to keep up. She would never get used to the crowds and the over-stimulating electronic advertisements on every building in Times Square. The vibrant city attracted people from all over the world and lived up to its reputation of being the city that never sleeps.

Peyton had been planning to visit New York City for years but had never found the time. No that wasn't true. She never made the time. Now she was glad she waited. Experiencing the city with Michael by her side would be better than traipsing around alone.

"You okay?" Michael released her hand and wrapped his arm around her once they made it to a portion of the sidewalk that wasn't as crowded.

"I'm fine now that you've slowed down. For a minute there I felt as if we were running from some bad guys."

Michael laughed. "Sorry about that. It was either bogard our way through the crowd or get stuck." He kissed the side of her head and heat soared through her body. Throughout the evening, she kept stealing glances at him, finding it hard to believe they were there together. So many days she thought about him, wondering what he was up to and if he was thinking about her. She was only in town for five days and planned to make the best of her time there.

Michael directed her down a side street that wasn't well lit, his attention on their surroundings. Like the street they had just left, this one was just as crowded. They passed several small theaters and eateries, everyone seeming to have a good time with no intentions of retiring for the night.

"What did you think of the restaurant and club?" Michael asked when they cleared another batch of people huddled on the sidewalk.

"The food was outstanding. I've had chicken and waffles before, but those were the best I've ever had. As for the show, I never heard of the performer, but the tribute he did to Prince was on point."

"I saw how you were all into the show when he sang *Adore*. For a minute there, I thought you were going to go up on stage and join him."

Peyton laughed and swatted his arm. "I wasn't that bad. You have to admit, if you weren't looking at the stage, you would have thought Prince himself was up there singing."

Michael nodded, smiling. "Yeah, you're right."

"And who knew you could sing? You've been holding out."

"What can I say, there's a lot you don't know about me yet." He wiggled his eyebrows and flaunted that wicked grin that sent a delicious quiver raking over her flesh.

Peyton wrapped her arm around his waist. "Well, you can sing for me anytime, and I look forward to learning more about you." He pulled her closer and kissed her lips.

They arrived at her hotel ten minutes later and stepped onto the elevator after three other people. Peyton pushed the button for her floor and stepped back, bumping into Michael.

"Sorry."

"No problem."

She took a step, but he held her in place, an arm around her waist, and a hand resting on her left hip. Awareness of his closeness hummed through her, and she leaned into him. His hard body felt too good to move away.

Peyton wasn't ready for the evening to end. She

respected his decision to stay clear of a serious relationship, but she wanted him if only for one night. All she had to do was convince him that she could handle a one-night stand.

*

To stay or not to stay was the question rattling around in Michael's head. He didn't have to rush home since his parents were with Michaela and he wasn't ready to say good night. But he also didn't think it was a good idea to follow Peyton inside of her hotel room. Whatever was happening between them was strong, and clearly she felt the connection too. However, for his own peace of mind, he had to make sure she was ready. He had to make sure they both were ready.

When Peyton unlocked the door and pushed it open, Michael grabbed her arm, stopping her from going inside.

She frowned. "Aren't you coming in?"

"What do you have planned for tomorrow?" he asked instead of answering her question.

She studied him before speaking. "Sightseeing. Since this is my first time in New York, I have a list of places I want to visit. I plan to see everything." She slid her hands inside of his jacket, her fingers crawling up his chest. She leaned closer, their lips almost touching. "And I mean *everything.*"

Michael smiled. He wasn't the only one ready to take what was building between them to the next level. But he knew her. Tough and sassy one minute, soft and vulnerable the next. The emotional damage her ex-husband inflicted on her went deep. She was talking tough now, but if he couldn't give her the type of relationship she desired, that hole in her heart would only grow bigger. Besides that, there were things she didn't know about him, things he needed to tell her before they went any further.

"How about I show you around tomorrow? Take you to some of the main attractions and help you cross a few items off your list. Who knows, you might be able to see *everything* you want to see," he said pointedly, giving her a quick peck on the lips. But the way she stared up at him with those big brown eyes, something within him stirred. A combination of desire and fear battled inside of him. He wanted to do right by her but...

Michael crushed her to him, pressing his mouth over hers and stabbing her lips apart with his tongue. Hot and searing. He'd had a semi-erection most of the night thinking about all the ways he wanted to make love to her. But right now he just wanted to taste her.

Desire rocked through him as their kiss went from zero to sixty in intensity, sending a shock wave of need straight to his groin. He backed her against the wall and rubbed his body against hers, needing Peyton to feel how much he wanted her, desired her. Michael moaned into her mouth when she fisted the front of his shirt in her hands and ground against his erection.

"Shit." He groaned in frustration, his body battling with his mind. While his body begged to take what they'd started into the room, his mind insisted – not yet.

He eased his mouth from hers, both his hands now cupping her butt as he kissed her cheek and worked his way down to her neck. He ached with need. This would be the last time. This would be the last time they kissed like that and not end up in bed together.

Soon, but not tonight.

"I have to go," he said, his voice husky as he worked to get his body under control. "I don't want to, but I think it's best."

"Michael, you don't have to go."

Sharon C. Cooper

"Yes, I do."

Peyton blew out a breath and pushed him, bumping into the door in the process.

"If this is you being a gentleman, stop it!" She snapped. He chuckled unable to help himself. Seeming to piss her off more. "You don't have to handle me like…like I might break. If you don't want me, dammit just tell me. Don't keep getting me all worked up only to walk away."

The smile fell from his lips. He closed the distance between them and cupped her cheek.

"Baby, I want you more than I have wanted anyone in my entire life. Don't ever doubt that I want you." He dropped his hand and ran it over his head, uncertainty charging through his body. "My hesitation is not about you. This is all me." He pounded his chest, pissed that he'd given her doubt about how much he wanted her.

Peyton ran her hands over his abs. Michael sucked in a ragged breath. *Again with those damn hands.* Her gentle touch sent erotic waves through his shirt and to his body. Her fingers did a slow, excruciating crawl up his torso and didn't stop moving until they rested on his chest. And those lips. Those sweet, plump lips only a whisper away from his, had him damn near panting.

It wasn't until she met his gaze did he slowly release the breath he'd been holding.

"I know you're not looking for anything serious. I get that. But we're both adults. We can hit the sheets tonight and still be friends tomorrow."

Michael chuckled, despite how the rhythm of his heartbeat increased in tempo with her touch and the seduction of her voice. "You're sexy as hell when you talk like that, but…we need to talk."

"We can talk later."

He cupped her face between his hands. "Baby, I don't want to hurt you."

She searched his eyes and then moved her mouth even closer. "You won't."

A low growl rumbled in Michael's throat when her lips met his. How the hell was he supposed to resist her when she swirled her tongue around his? "God, I want you," he mumbled against her mouth and squeezed her butt.

"Prove it."

Chapter Eleven

Michael had Peyton in the room and out of their clothes in record time. And like in Jamaica, her heart thundered at the sight of his naked, tattooed body. His muscular form on full display.

Perfection.

Of all the words in the English dictionary, that was the only one to best describe the magnificence of his toned body.

"You're even more beautiful than I remember." Michael's raspy tone snagged her attention, sending goosebumps prickling up her arms. His admiring gaze did a slow stroll down her body as he eased toward her, ripping the silver packet open with his teeth. "You teased me mercilessly with these big, beautiful breasts of yours weeks ago. Breasts that have filled my nightly dreams since our time in Jamaica. Now I plan to enjoy them and every inch of your body."

Her gaze slid to his long, thick erection as he quickly sheathed himself. Peyton swallowed, her heart pounding loud enough for the people in the room next door to hear.

"You told me to prove how much I want you." The bass in his voice dropped an octave as he backed her to a nearby wall. "I plan to prove how much I want you, over and over again."

Peyton shrieked when he gripped the back of her thighs and lifted her, the tip of her nipple in line with his lips. His tongue shot out, swirled around the sensitive bud, sending a blast of heat shooting to the center of her core. Her eyes slammed closed at the delicious warmth consuming her body.

"Michael," she whimpered. He paid the same homage to the other nipple, gently sucking, bracing her against the wall as if she weighed nothing. The throbbing ache between Peyton's thighs grew more intense when her legs went around his waist, and she ground her pelvis against his muscular abs.

"Mmm, Peyton, baby..." Michael said in a gruff whisper, his hold on her tightened as he lowered her body, positioning her just right to feel his erection against her throbbing sex. She trembled in his arms when the tip of his penis teased the opening at the apex of her thighs.

A moan pierced the air and Peyton wasn't sure if it came from herself or Michael. At the moment, she didn't care. All she wanted was to feel more of him.

Michael slid into her, and Peyton's mouth formed a perfect "o" as her breath caught in her lungs. All rational thought flew from her mind. Her arms tightened around his shoulders as he moved, rotating his hips ever so slowly, giving her body a chance to adjust around his thick shaft.

"You okay?" he asked, his words filled with a thickness she'd never heard from him before.

She leaned back, her head against the wall, and their

gazes colliding. Their eyes did the talking for them as he picked up speed sliding in and out of her, never breaking eye contact. He lifted her slightly, sliding her up and down his length.

In and out. Faster. Deeper. Harder.

As if a switch had been flipped on, his moves got even faster, jerkier. Peyton's pulse pounded loudly in her ears, and her heart rate kicked up as a pool of ecstasy viciously whirled around inside of her.

"Michael, Michael, Mi…" The breathy chant of his name tumbled from her mouth with every powerful thrust until… "Michael!" she screamed, her nails digging into his bare shoulders as she bucked and jerked against him. He slammed inside of her faster, harder. Wave, after wave of pleasure thrashed against every cell in her body, jostling and twisting within her, sending her over the edge of reality.

Michael was right behind her, growling his release, his fingers digging into the back of her thighs as he held her tightly.

"Ahh, shiiiiitttt!" He crushed her against the wall, their hearts feeling as if they were beating as one against Peyton's chest. "Ahh, ba…baby," he panted loudly against her sweat-slicked shoulder, readjusting his hold on the back of her thighs.

Neither spoke or moved for the longest time. Not until Michael huffed out a breath and suddenly lifted her higher in his arms, stumbling to the bed. He practically dropped her onto it and leaned over her, his hands braced on the mattress, his breathing still uneven.

"I'll be right back." He pecked her lips and staggered to the bathroom.

*

Michael returned to the room and dug through his

pocket for his wallet, hoping he had another condom. Finding his emergency one, he tossed it to the bedside table. Now that he'd had Peyton, he wanted more. That little taste had gone way too fast. The next time, he wanted to take his time.

Climbing onto the bed, Michael pulled Peyton into his arms. She stared up at him. Those dreamy eyes and a wicked smile on her lips had his shaft stirring again.

"You proved your point," she said with a nervous chuckle. "Man, that was—"

"Incredible," he finished. "Just like you." Michael nibbled her top lip before sliding a greedy tongue into her mouth, lapping up every bit of her sweetness. What they had shared exceeded his expectations, and he wanted more, much, much more.

As if reading his mind, Peyton pulled her mouth from his and leaned up on her elbow. Michael watched through lowered lashes as she first tweaked his nipple between her fingers before lowering her head. A tingling sensation shot through his body to the tips of his toes when her teeth grazed over the hardened peak. Her small hand caressed his chest, moving in small circles to match the swirl of her tongue against his nipple and then her hand moved lower.

Michael swallowed hard, and he gripped the back of her head lightly when she coiled her hand around his shaft. His eyes drifted closed. Blood rushed from his brain and shot straight to his groin. His penis pulsed with every stroke of her hand along his length.

"Ahh...baby." His throaty groan seemed to spur her on, and his grip tightened in her hair. His body pumped in tuned with each stroke as she slid her hand up and down the smoothness of his shaft. "Pe..." he sputtered when she squeezed, her hand moving faster, and faster.

Her grip tightened, but she kept the pace, intermittently rubbing her thumb over the tip.

"You like that?" she crooned, warmth spreading throughout his body.

"Shit...ye...yeah, but...shi..." he growled, the rest of the curse dropping off when he bolted upright, covering her hand to stop her movements. "I liked." He wheezed. "I liked it too much."

Michael snatched the foil packet from the bed table and hurried to sheathed himself. *So much for taking this round slow.* The way she had his body on fire, there was no way in hell he could take this slow.

He turned to lay Peyton on her back, but she stopped him with a hand to his chest, shaking her head.

"I'm on top." She pushed him back and straddled him.

Michael couldn't stop the huge smile that spread across his lips. "Whatever you say, Boss Lady. Go ahead. Have your way with me."

*

"This is spectacular." Peyton leaned into Michael. "Seeing Central Park on television and in the movies is nothing compared to experiencing it in person."

They were in a horse drawn carriage on a guided tour of the famous park. Though the trees were barren and some patches of the grass were brown, the park was still as beautiful as Peyton imagined. Couples strolled hand in hand along the path as if they weren't in a hurry to get anywhere, while others biked or skated, despite the chill in the air.

"Yeah, hanging out here never gets old," Michael said as the tour guide pointed toward the area where the zoo was located. Michael's arm tightened around Peyton when she shivered from the light breeze. The temperature had warmed up from the night before, but at fifty-five degrees, it was still chilly. "This is my first time taking a carriage ride. Normally I walk."

"So you're having another first with me today, huh?" Peyton glanced up at Michael, his heated gaze on her. Warmth spread through her body and a smile tugged on the corner of her lips.

"I have a few more *firsts* with you planned for today."

His mouth touched hers. The kiss, soft and sweet, only increased the sexual tension that had intensified since their night together.

He pulled her closer, deepening the kiss, his tongue dipping in and out of her mouth sending tingles through her body. Their tongue aerobics had her wanting to climb onto his lap and go much farther than kissing. Normally, she didn't venture off the straight and narrow path, not interested in taking many chances or doing anything that might hurt her physically or emotionally. But Michael made her want to live on the edge and throw caution out the window for a chance at happiness, a chance to experience life on different terms.

Michael had spent the night. Since he kept a spare change of clothes in his vehicle, he didn't have to go home to change before touring around town with her. Peyton enjoyed their day visiting Grand Central Station, Bryant Park, Rockefeller Center, and hopefully the final stop Central Park. Now all she wanted was to go back to his place, make love and lay wrapped in his strong arms.

The stolen kisses, affectionate gazes, and the flirting they'd done throughout the day only made her hornier.

"Your kisses are addictive. I can't get enough," Michael mumbled against her lips, his voice thick with arousal. His intense gaze had her trembling against him. "How about we make this our last tourist attraction for today?"

Peyton studied him, glad they seemed to be on the same page. "I think that's a good idea."

Night had fallen by the time they walked back to the parking garage where Michael had left his SUV earlier that morning. They were heading to his home in Brooklyn and Peyton trembled in her seat. She wasn't cold. Anticipation had her practically jumping out of her skin. Michael had insisted that she check out of the hotel and spend the rest of her trip with him.

No strings attached was what she kept telling herself throughout the day. His comments in Jamaica about not being the committed or relationship type kept playing in her head. People indulged in flings all the time, surely she could too. She had to. Making love to him the night before had only wet her appetite.

Michael reached over and squeezed her thigh. "We won't do anything you don't want to do."

Apparently, he took her eagerness as nervousness. "As long as it's with you, I want to do everything you have in mind." She had never flirted or been so bold with a man, not even her ex-husband, but this felt right. She didn't necessarily believe in kindred spirits or soul mates, but there was something special between her and Michael that couldn't be ignored.

"I never told you this, but your quick comebacks are a serious turn on."

Peyton grinned, feeling pretty proud of herself that she could still turn a man on. "Well, I hope there's more about me that turns you on."

"Hell yeah, baby. Everything about you turns me on. I'm looking forward to our plans for tonight."

"You didn't let me in on what you have in mind. Technically they're your plans."

He laughed. "That's right. They are my plans aren't

they?" He lifted her hand to his mouth, placing a kiss inside her palm. "Well, I have big plans for you tonight."

His voice dropped an octave and Peyton's pulse kicked up, a tremor shooting through her body. She didn't know what he had in store for her, but she had every intention of going with the flow.

Michael released her hand and turned a corner, street lamps casting light against brownstones that lined the street. Like Central Park, Peyton had seen her share of New York brownstones on television or heard about them in books, now she saw them first hand. Some were a bit rundown, but that didn't take away from the architectural detail, at least from what she could make out in the dimness of the night.

Her cell phone rang and she dug it out of the side of her handbag. *Dylan.* That was the third time he'd called that day. As with the night before, he hadn't left a message.

"Hello," she answered, curious about the calls.

"Hey, do you have time to talk?"

"Not really," she said carefully, thinking that maybe she shouldn't have answered with Michael sitting next to her. They might have been only friends, but it still seemed weird to have a conversation with her ex-husband while she was with Michael.

"Please, PJ. It's important. Discussing this on the phone is not a good idea. Can we meet somewhere?"

"No. I'm not in Cincinnati. What is this about?"

"Where are you?"

"That's none of your business. What is so important that you have to keep calling me?" Now he had her curious. She hadn't heard from him in years and all of sudden he was sending her flowers and calling.

"When will you be back in Cincinnati?"

"Dylan, I'm not answering any of your questions if you refuse to answer mine."

"I just...I want to talk to you face to face. I miss you, Peyton."

She pulled the phone away from her ear and stared at it not expecting his declaration. There was no way that was what he was calling for. He hadn't given a damn about her when they were married and all of sudden he missed her?

She disconnected the call and turned off the phone, dropping it in the side pocket of her handbag. Disgust churned in her gut thinking about how he had mistreated her, disrespecting her and their marriage. There was nothing he could say that would stop her from seeing him as the lowest form of human life.

"You alright?" Michael asked.

"I'm fine!" she snapped. Catching herself, she dialed back the attitude. No way was she going to take her dislike of Dylan out on Michael. "Sorry."

Michael didn't say anything. He pulled up next to a car, his arm on the back of her seat as he glanced out of the window to parallel park.

"Is that your home?" Peyton pointed to the brownstone they were parked in front of, vines crawling up the front of the structure.

"No. We passed it, about a block back. Hopefully, you can handle a little more walking."

"Definitely." She unhooked her seatbelt, but Michael halted her, his hand covering hers.

"What's going on with your ex? I assume his phone calls are the ones you've been trying to ignore all day."

Peyton stared into his eyes, not surprised that he had noticed her annoyance whenever her phone rang, and she saw Dylan's name on the screen.

"Nothing's going on. He started calling a couple of weeks ago wanting to talk." Peyton turned her hand over, linking her fingers with Michael's. "I shouldn't have answered, especially since I'm not interested in talking to him. I'm here with you, right where I want to be." She tugged his hand, pulling him close to kiss him.

"Are you sure you're okay staying with me for the rest of your trip, Peyton?" he asked when they pulled apart.

"Positive. So you gon' take me to your house or what?"

Michael laughed and climbed out of the vehicle, jogging around to open the door for her. They retrieved her bags from the backseat and took the short walk to his house.

Peyton heard voices when they opened the exterior door and stood in the small foyer facing a glass door that led into the house. Michael had mentioned that his daughter was spending the next few days with his parents, but it sounded like they were still there.

He pushed the door open.

"Daddy!" a cute little girl with a thick ponytail bouncing from the top of her head screamed. She charged toward him and leaped. Michael caught her with one arm, and Peyton was convinced they had the routine down.

"Hey, Baby Doll." He set Peyton's suitcase down near a set of stairs and placed a noisy kiss on his daughter's cheek, hugging her tight. Peyton set the small carry on, she'd been holding, next to the suitcase. The little girl eyed her over Michael's shoulder and smiled. The thought of dating a man with children didn't appeal to Peyton, but her heart squeezed at the sight of his daughter. Eyes and a grin so similar to Michael's, the little girl was adorable.

Michael set his daughter on her feet when an older

woman strolled from the back of the house drying her hands on a dishtowel.

"Peyton, this is Michaela, and that's my mother, Laura Cutter."

"Nice to meet you," his mother said shaking Peyton's hand.

"It's a pleasure to meet you, too."

"What about me?" Michaela jumped in front of Peyton, who laughed and extended her hand to the little girl.

"It's nice to meet you as well." Michaela smiled, and Peyton's heart squeezed a little more. Maybe she'd been too hasty ruling out dating men with children.

"I had planned for us to be gone by the time you arrived," Mrs. Cutter said to Michael and cast a warm smile at Peyton.

"That's alright. I wanted you guys to meet Peyton anyway. So it worked out. Where's dad?" Michael asked of his stepfather.

"He ran to the store for me, but should be back in a minute and then we'll head out of here. Oh and there's dinner in the refrigerator."

"Okay. Thanks, Mom." Michael reached for Peyton's hand. "Come with me."

Michaela started after them, but her grandmother stopped her. "Michaela come back to the kitchen and finish eating, and then I need you to help Nana finish the dishes." Peyton heard the little girl grumble, but whatever else her grandmother said, worked. Michaela was no longer trailing behind them.

They went around the stairs and stopped in a short hallway. When his mother and daughter were out of earshot, Michael backed Peyton against a closet door. He seized her lips before she formed her next thought and she gasped in surprise, but quickly recovered. She could easily get used to his delicious kisses. For years, she'd waited for a man who stirred the type of passion within her that Michael aroused, and he didn't disappoint.

"Daddy?" Michaela called out.

Michael growled and rested his forehead against Peyton's. "I'll get rid of them." He winked. "But first, let me hang up your coat." After placing their garments in the closet, they strolled back the way they came and headed to the kitchen.

Peyton admired Michael's home. The hardwood floors looked to be original to the house. Her gaze took in the impressive chandelier at the entrance, double crown molding, and the arch that led into a large great room. The space was sparsely decorated, with only a huge sofa facing the fireplace. What the house lacked in furnishings and wall décor, it made up in character and architectural detail.

"You have a beautiful home," Peyton said as he pulled her along.

"Thank you."

When they made it to the kitchen, he directed her to one of the high-back barstools next to the counter. "Are you hungry? Thirsty?"

"I could go for some water."

"Coming right up."

While in Jamaica, Michael had told her that the brownstone was a fixer-upper when he purchased the property. Peyton could tell where he was still renovating. Though there were top of the line appliances and fixtures, cabinets had been removed from some walls, revealing mismatched paint colors in some spots.

"Daddy, can I stay here with you and Peyton?"

"I'm back." A deep, sing-song voice came from the

front of the house.

Michaela's eyes grew wide. "Papa!" She took off in a sprint out of the room and Michael shook his head.

"Clearly she doesn't understand the phrase 'no running in the house'," Michael grumbled.

"Peyton's here. I'm staying with her and daddy." Peyton heard Michaela say when she appeared in the doorway in the arms of a giant of a man.

"Michaela, you're going home with us," Mrs. Cutter said placing a plate in the upper cabinet near the sink.

Michaela's lips turned down, and she folded her arms.

"Michaela, we're not doing this tonight. You're going home with Nana and Papa. What's going on, Dad?" Michael fist-bumped his father.

"Not much, son."

"Let me introduce you. Dad, this is Peyton Jenkins. Peyton, this is my father, Carlton Cutter."

The admiration Peyton heard in Michael's voice didn't go unnoticed. Whatever Carlton had done for him had earned his stepson's respect.

Carlton set Michaela on her feet, and a tremor shot through Peyton when his gaze met hers. Taller than Michael by a few inches, Carlton was also wider across the shoulders. No doubt when he was a cop, intimidating perps probably came easy. His intense dark eyes bore into her, but when he smiled, the crinkles at the corner of his eyes softened his features.

"Pleasure to meet you, Peyton."

"Nice to meet you too, Mr. Cutter."

"Call me Carlton. We keep things pretty informal around here."

Peyton shook his hand thinking that a recruiter for a voice-over artist would kill for a client like Carlton whose deep, bass-baritone sounded so much like Barry White.

"Welcome to New York. I hope you're enjoying your visit," Carlton said.

Her gaze met Michael's. "Thank you. So far I'm having a great time."

Michael winked at her and an unexpected warmth pooled at the center of her core making it almost unbearable to stand still. She didn't know what all he had planned for the evening, but she couldn't wait to find out.

Michael's cell phone rang. "Excuse me for a minute. I need to take this." He handed Peyton a bottle of water and squeezed her shoulder on his way out of the room.

Peyton sipped from the bottle, her hands shaking slightly. She hadn't met a man's family in a long time and forgot how awkward it could be.

"Michael mentioned earlier that you two were going to tour Manhattan. How did it go?" Carlton sat at the small glass table where Michaela was eating chicken fingers.

"From what I've seen of New York so far, I love it. I think Central Park and Times Square are my favorite. The energy of the city is very different from what I'm used to in Cincinnati, but I don't know if I would ever get used to so many people."

Laura flashed that same warm smile as earlier. "I know what you mean, but the other boroughs aren't as congested as Manhattan. I've lived in New York my whole life and despite the number of people, I don't think I could ever live anywhere else in the country. Like you, I love the energy of Manhattan and there's always so much to do."

They discussed some of the sites that Peyton had visited and talked a little about her work in Cincinnati. As with conversation with Michael, Peyton found it easy to talk to his parents. Laura had a similar sense of humor as her son that immediately put Peyton at ease.

"Dad, can you come here for a minute?" Michael called from the other room, and Carlton excused himself.

Peyton took another sip from the bottled water when there was a lull in the conversation and glanced across the room at Michaela. She finished her dinner and handed her plate to Laura before strolling around the counter to Peyton.

"Are you my daddy's girlfriend?"

Peyton sputtered and coughed, her water going down wrong. She stood patting her chest, trying to catch her breath, tears clouding her eyes.

"Michaela, what did I tell you before your daddy and Peyton got here?" Laura whispered loud enough for Peyton to hear as she moved Michaela back toward the round kitchen table.

"Are you okay?" Laura came up behind Peyton, rubbing her back.

Peyton nodded, still coughing and unable to speak.

Michael re-entered the kitchen, stuffing his phone into his pant pocket. His gaze met Peyton's and his brows dipped into a frown.

"What's wrong?" He walked over and cupped her cheek, concern swimming in his eyes. No doubt she was probably beet red, a disadvantage of having such fair skin. "What happened?"

"Nothing, my water just went down wrong." Peyton used the back of her hand to wipe her eyes. When he didn't look convinced, she added, "I'm fine, and Michaela, your daddy and I are just friends."

"Oh," she said as if disappointed. Michael turned to his daughter, but before he could say anything Michaela said, "Uncle Shon said Daddy needs to get laid and—"

"Michaela!" Michael and his mother said in unison, both looking as if they wanted to place tape over the little girl's mouth.

Michael shook his head and rubbed his eyes. "Wait until I get my hands on that..." his voice trailed off, and he released a noisy sigh.

"Michaela, go and get your bag. We need to get going," Carlton said walking back into the kitchen. Apparently he had heard his granddaughter. His exasperated expression matched Michael's and Laura's.

"Papa, I don't want to go. I want to stay with Daddy and Peyton," Michaela said to Carlton, but huddled up to Michael, her little arms around his leg.

"Michaela, we talked about this. You're staying with Nana and Papa tonight and tomorrow. Remember?"

She pouted more and didn't respond.

"Go and get your bag now," Michael said, his tone firm, leaving no room for argument.

Michaela looked up, her teary-eyed gaze bouncing from him to Peyton and back again.

"Can I show Peyton my room first? Pleeeease?"

Peyton had to give Michaela credit for her stall technique.

"What did I te—"

"I would love to see your room," Peyton interrupted and gave Michael a slight shrug. She didn't know how he could say no to Michaela's sweet little face.

Michael hesitated, and Peyton saw the smile on his mother's face as she turned to busy herself wiping down the kitchen counter.

"Five minutes, Michaela, then you're outta here." Michael directed the words at Michaela, but his gaze was on Peyton. She read him loud and clear.

Thirty minutes later, Michael locked the front door, set the alarm, and turned to Peyton. "I have waited all day to have you all to myself."

Peyton smiled and moved toward him. This had been one of the best days she'd had in a long time. Spending the day with him and then meeting his family felt normal. And she was in love with Michaela. The little girl had a big personality to be so young. She reminded Peyton of Martina, saying whatever was on her mind.

"Now that you have me to yourself, what are you going to do with me?"

Michael gave her a quick kiss, then held her hand and headed to the kitchen, turning off lights along the way.

Giddiness bubbled inside of her, but she reminded herself that though they were spending the next few days together, it didn't mean a lifetime commitment. She was okay with that. They were both consenting adults about to have some fun.

Michael released her hand and opened the refrigerator, pulling out a can of whipped cream.

Adrenaline soared through Peyton's veins in anticipation of his plans. While married, she and Dylan rarely tried anything new in the bedroom and right now, Peyton was willing to try just about anything with Michael. "Um…I'm almost afraid to ask what you have in mind."

"Get your head out of the gutter, woman." Michael laughed and reached back into the refrigerator. "I just needed something to go with the strawberries." He held them up for her to see.

"Oh." Peyton was sure the heat flushing her face had her looking like a bright red tomato. Michael was the adventurous type, and she assumed that when he said he had big plans for her that evening, it would probably involve something freakier than the night before.

Michael set the items down and locked Peyton in place against the counter, his powerful arms on each side of her. "I'm..." He kissed the tip of her nose. "Just..." He kissed her cheek. "Messing with you." The feathery touch of his lips on hers tantalized every nerve in her body, and she would have puddled to the floor had he not placed a hand on her hip. Mumbling against her mouth, he said, "I plan to make this a night you'll remember, whipped cream and all."

Chapter Twelve

Minutes later, Michael handed Peyton the whipped cream and strawberries while he climbed the stairs with her luggage. He couldn't wait to get Peyton naked and into his bed, and not necessarily in that order.

Michael guided her down the hallway to his bedroom and pushed open the door. Setting her bags inside the room, he flipped the two switches against the wall. One bathed the room with dim lighting from the bedside table lamps. The other controlled the room's audio system. The sound of Boney James melodic saxophone flowed softly around the room through the hidden speakers in the ceiling.

"Come on in and make yourself comfortable."

Peyton set the props next to the lamp on the bedside table, closest to the door, and slowly glanced around the space. "This room is huge. Ohhh and you have a fireplace. I've always wanted one in my bedroom." The awe in her voice had him sticking his chest out more, glad that she liked the space that was probably more masculine than she was accustomed to. His large, king sized bed made of a dark cherry wood, took up much of the space. A small reading area, comprised of his favorite wide chair and a round table, sat near the fireplace.

"I'll get us a fire going and warm it up in here," Michael said when Peyton stepped away from the fireplace and roamed around the bedroom, studying the artwork he had on the walls. Michael bent to place a log in the fireplace.

A slight tremble of his hands when he added the log, had him chuckling to himself. This was the first time he'd ever brought a woman to his home, and never had one shared his bed. Not even Octavia. He preferred to go to a woman's place not only because of Michaela but because he didn't want any woman getting too comfortable in his space. But Peyton wasn't just any woman. He knew there was something special about her from the moment they met.

Michael pulled the flimsy fireplace screen together and stood. "If you want, you ca…" His words lodged inside of his throat when he turned to find Peyton stretched out on his bed in the skimpiest bra and panty set he'd ever seen on a woman.

"You said to make myself comfortable." The sexy purr of her voice had him lifting his T-shirt over his head and tossing it to the floor.

"I did, didn't I?" He toed off his left boot and then his right, glad he never bothered tying up the footwear. His gaze took in the lacy, pink bra showcasing Peyton's bountiful breasts and the little strip of material masquerading as panties.

Peyton sat forward and unhooked the bra, tossing the pink lace dramatically to the floor on the side of the bed. She went for her undies.

"Stop." Peyton's hands stilled on the band of her

panties. "You gotta save something for me to do, baby."

Michael hurried, his heart rate kicking up a notch as he hastily removed his jeans. Tossing them into the heap he'd created with his other clothes, he crawled onto the bed, clad in only his boxer briefs.

Michael took his time and eased the tiny lace down Peyton's long, shapely legs and brought the panties to his nose, inhaling the erotic scent as his gaze locked onto hers. The right corner of her lips lifted and Michael's penis leaped to attention.

Damn. This woman. This incredibly sexy woman had him all twisted up inside. He set the undies aside and grabbed the can of whipped cream from the table, shaking it.

"You look so good. I can't decide where to start." He hovered above Peyton, his gaze on her perky breasts. He was definitely a breasts man.

Michael straddled Peyton, shaking the can more and grinning when she shivered beneath him.

She placed her hands against his chest and laughed. "Michael, I don't know about this."

He grabbed her wrists in his large hands and held them above her head. Not giving her a chance to say anything, he squeezed the tip of the can, creating a circle of whip cream over one of her nipples.

Peyton bucked under him. "Oh my God! Michael!" She giggled, wiggling beneath him, her pelvis bumping against his erection, sending a shiver through his body. "That's co...cold."

"You keep moving like that, and this is going to be over way too fast," he ground out, his shaft growing thicker, straining against his briefs.

Wanting to finish what he'd started, Michael covered the other perky peak, eliciting the same reaction from

Peyton, but ignoring her protests. He lowered his head and slid his tongue around her nipple, her sweetness blending with that of the cream.

Peyton's sexy moans mingling with the soft jazz, had Michael dropping the can next to them thinking he'd have to get to the strawberries later. He lifted one of her hips, grinding hard against her, knowing that he was playing with fire. He bit down lightly on her nipple, and she purred, a sound that he was quickly getting used to.

"Michael," she whimpered, pulling her hands from his grip and holding the back of his head as she continued squirming, her moans growing louder.

Michael worshiped the other nipple, taking his time cleaning off the cream with slow, sweeping strokes of his tongue. He would have kept going had her hands not moved to his ass, and she ground harder against him.

Peyton's nipple plopped from his mouth, and Michael covered her lips with his, growling against them. Her erotic moans were like fuel, stoking the wildfire burning inside of him and his defenses were no match for the power she had over him. His tongue did a hungry exploration, ravishing her mouth as his arousal inched higher and higher, but it wasn't enough.

Michael snatched his mouth from hers and gripped her hips, stilling her in place, his shaft throbbing with need. "I wanted to take this slow, baby, but—"

"Next time. You can go slow next time." She cupped his package and squeezed, prompting curses to fly from his mouth, and pure pleasure gripped his body.

"Ahh, hell." He lifted up and stripped out of his briefs. He opened the drawer on the side of the bed and grabbed a condom, quickly sheathing himself. "You're too damn much for me," he grumbled when he nudged her legs wider with his knees.

Michael entered her, and it was if he had arrived home after a long trip. Peyton cried out and tightened around him. Michael froze. Fear gripped his body. "Did I hurt—"

"Don't stop. Baby, please don't stop." Peyton grasped his butt, forcing him to slide up and down, and in and out of her tightness. Michael squeezed her hips, fighting against the need to take her quicker. But Peyton's slick heat enveloped him like a thick blanket, warming him from the inside out.

Michael knew he couldn't take much more of this. He increased his pace and Peyton matched him, stroke for stroke, pulling him deeper into her sweet heat. Michael groaned, gritting his teeth, trying to hold onto the little control he had left, but loving the friction of her body rubbed up against his.

Peyton's legs wrapped around his waist, and he pounded into her faster and harder, his hands slipping on her sweat, slicked thighs.

"Michael!" Peyton hoarse cry rang out near his ear, as she squeezed his biceps, crumbling in his arms. Michael loved hearing her scream his name.

A few more hard thrusts and he stiffened. His body tightened as an orgasm ripped through him, sending a growl from the pit of his stomach rushing out of his mouth as his world spun out of control.

He collapsed on top of her, his eyes tightly closed as he fought to catch his breath. Hearing Peyton panting near his ear, he quickly lifted, not wanting to crush her. The sticky whipped cream residue on her breasts stuck to him. A reminder that he never got to finish what he'd started.

Michael rolled to his back, pulling Peyton against his side. They lay gasping for air, and Michael chuckled. "I think you're trying to kill me."

"Me?" she wheezed. "You're the one doing wicked things with whipped cream and your tongue."

"I…I couldn't help it. Your breasts tempt me in ways I can't even explain."

"Good. I like being able to tempt you."

"And you do it so well." Michael tweaked her nipple, and she yelped, swiping his hand away. He pulled her on top of him. "I love playing with you. Next time – wait 'til you see what I can do with strawberries."

*

Hours later, Michael returned to the bed and pulled Peyton into his arms, kissing the top of her head. Sated, they lay quietly in the dimly lit room, wood crackling in the fireplace and the smooth sounds of Najee playing through the room's speakers.

Peyton snuggled closer, her leg draped over his thigh and her small hand resting on his chest. This felt right. Hell, everything about his time with her felt right.

"What are you thinking about?" she asked.

"When we were in Jamaica, you asked me about the long scar on my neck," Michael started, knowing it was past time for him to tell her his story.

"I remember," Peyton said quietly, her fingers tracing a path along the scar.

He covered her hand, drawing strength from her to discuss something he rarely shared with anyone.

"I was cut with a broken bottle during a bar fight. I'd had a little too much to drink. Add that to my cocky attitude and you have a bad combination." He had blocked so many of the details of that evening out, but there was so much of his life he wished he could erase from his memory. "I was meeting, Octavia, Michaela's mom there with the intention of ending our relationship."

Peyton lifted her head, her brows raised. "At a bar?"

He shrugged. "What can I say? I made a lot of poor decisions that night."

She rested her head against his shoulder. In hindsight, maybe telling Peyton about that time in his life might not be the best idea. But this was a conversation they needed to have at some point. After spending the last couple of days with her, Michael wanted her in his life in some capacity. He wanted unconditional love. Someone he could depend on. A person who trusted him enough to depend on him. He wanted what Luke and Christina had found in each other. He wanted what his stepfather and his mother had.

Part of Michael could see spending his life with Peyton. Would she be able to handle the baggage from his past? More importantly, was he ready to give her the type of relationship and commitment she wanted? Could he be the man she deserved?

He let those questions marinate in his mind. Maybe they could just play that part of their relationship by ear. Michael had no intention of dating anyone else, and he knew Peyton was a one-man woman. Besides, they'd only known each other a month. It was too early to be thinking about commitments anyway.

Peyton lifted up on her elbow. "What led to the fight?" Staring into her caring eyes gave him the encouragement needed to continue.

"I've always had a short fuse when it comes to men putting their hands on women or children. And that night..."

Trepidation churned in his gut and Michael lifted his gaze to the tray ceiling above his king sized bed. "Let me back up a little." He ran a nervous hand back and forth over his forehead as he gathered his thoughts. "Growing up, I watched my biological father, Lewis, use my mother's face and body as a punching bag. He was abusive just like his father had been. For years, I was afraid for my mother and me. I thought for sure I'd come home one day from school and find her dead."

"Oh, Michael." Peyton placed a kiss on his shoulder and another on his lips. She draped her arm across his chest, her body partially covering his as she embraced him. Michael found comfort in the simple move. As if she were somehow telling him, without saying the words, that he was safe.

Michael's gaze returned to the ceiling, as he debated how much to tell Peyton about his parents. His chest tightened at the memory of the last fight between them.

"The last time I saw Lewis was the day I called 911 because I thought he had killed my mother. I found him leaning over her, his hands around her neck and blood seeping from a gash on the side of her head."

Peyton gasped. "Oh my God." She leaned back to look at him. "What did you do?"

Tension coiled through Michael's body, gripping him like a metal vise around his neck. It was as if he was back in that living room, reliving every detail. Terror rioted through him at the sight of his mother's blood painting the carpet red. Even now he could smell Lewis reeking of urine, and stale beer mixed with sweat. He could see the crimson color on his father's hands supporting the evidence of what that monster had done.

"I hit him on the back of the head with a lamp. After I pushed him off of my mother, I called 911. I had just turned nine and was scared to death that my mother was dead and that I had killed Lewis." Michael glanced down, realizing his hands were balled into a fist. He opened and closed them several times, releasing some of the tightness in his body.

He sat up straighter, forcing Peyton to do the same when he leaned against the headboard, the large pillows supporting his back. He pulled Peyton against him, and she tugged the sheet up higher over her naked body.

Michael gathered his thoughts and continued, forcing himself to tell Peyton everything.

"Carlton was one of the responding officers."

"Was that your first time meeting, Carlton?"

Michael nodded.

"When they got there, was Lewis—"

"Passed out drunk with a gash on the back of his head from where I had hit him. Carlton told me that Lewis was probably too drunk to feel any pain."

"Did they arrest him?"

Michael hesitated. "My mother agreed not to press charges if he left us alone and never returned."

"Did he agree to her terms?"

"Yeah. He disappeared after that." For years, Michael didn't support his mother's decision. It wasn't until Carlton returned home one day and told them that Lewis had been found shot to death in Staten Island.

Peyton tried to hide a yawn, but failed, and Michael draped his arm around her. One o'clock in the morning wasn't the best time to talk about something so heavy, but when he'd tried to tell her about some of his past earlier that morning before checking out of the hotel, she didn't want to talk. She had pulled him into the shower with her, and suddenly he didn't want to talk either.

"Carlton stepped in once my father was out of the picture." Michael shook his head, shivering at what could have become of him had it not been for the man he now called Dad. "He saved my life...in more ways than one. I had been cutting up in school, but he wasn't having none of that. He told me I had to get my shit together."

Peyton leaned back to look at Michael. "And what did you do?"

Michael chuckled, a lightness coming over him as he remembered the early days with Carlton. "I got my shit together. You've seen him. Dude is huge, and he carried a gun."

Peyton laughed and snuggled back against Michael, listening as he explained about how well Carlton treated him and his mother.

"I wanted to be just like him."

As a decorated police officer, everyone on the police force looked up to Carlton and even after retiring, he was still held in high regard. Right out of high school, Michael had joined NYPD's police academy and was a cop for seven years, with every intention of being an officer until the day he retired. That was until the bar fight.

His heart hammered. Michael still needed to tell Peyton about the night at the bar, but with the story came even more information about him that he wanted to keep buried. If he didn't tell her, there was no chance of there ever being more between them.

"The abuse I witnessed stayed with me. Though I have never raised my hand to a woman like Lewis and his father did, there isn't a day that goes by that I don't fear that I might turn into them."

Peyton turned to him, holding the sheet to her chest. "Michael, I haven't known you that long, but you're nothing like them. You would never hurt a woman, and I believe that with all of my heart. You are the most thoughtful, gentlest man I have ever met."

Michael shook his head. "You might not think that when I tell you what happened during the bar fight." He threw off the covers and slipped on his boxer briefs before walking over to the sitting area near the fireplace. He couldn't continue with the story lying next to her.

Peyton watched him from across the room. He had no idea what she was thinking as she gathered up the bedding, covering herself even more. She stared at him without speaking.

Dropping down in one of the chairs, Michael rested his elbows on his thighs, rubbing his hands together trying to form the right words to tell his story. He glanced up and met Peyton's gaze.

"I'd had a couple of drinks before Octavia showed up, liquid courage in order to tell her that I couldn't do the whole relationship thing."

Peyton's eyes dimmed at his words. He'd given her a similar speech while in Jamaica.

"I guess I wasn't the only one with breaking news that night. Octavia told me she was pregnant. I didn't know what to think. Part of me thought she was lying, but I knew she had been sick for the two weeks leading up to that day. I just never imagined she could be pregnant."

Michael sat back in his seat and rubbed a shaky hand over his head. Peyton said nothing, her gaze steady on him as she waited patiently for him to finish.

"I needed space. Time to think. So I went outside for a smoke." Her brows lifted and he shrugged. "Oh yeah, I used to smoke too."

A slight smile graced her lips, and an invisible band tightened across Michael's chest, squeezing him. With every hour spent with her, she consumed a little more of his heart. He knew she was too good for him, but damn if he didn't still want her.

"What happened next?" she asked.

"When I went back into the bar, Octavia was still sitting at the table nursing a glass of water, but she wasn't alone. A guy was sitting across from her, getting all in her face. When she stood to leave, he blocked her path and grabbed her arm. Peyton, something inside of me snapped when he wouldn't release her. Everything after that happened so fast, I only remember bits and pieces. I yanked him away from her, telling him that she was with me and that he needed to respect a woman when she said no. We both had been drinking, but I do remember saying that."

Michael stood, unable to sit still any longer, anxiousness clawing inside of him. Telling the story to someone who meant more to him than he ever thought possible, had him worried. Maybe he was kidding himself thinking that he and Peyton could ever be anything more than friends.

"Tell me the rest," she said interrupting his musings.

"The guy broke a beer bottle. He swung his arm out and caught me just right, swiping the broken glass across my neck." Michael shook his head, guilt stabbing him in the heart. "Blood dripped down the front of my shirt and … I lost it. I slammed him against a wall and punched him, over and over and over. Before I knew it, I had the guy pinned to the ground, blood covering my hands. I didn't know if it was mine or his, but then he stopped moving."

"Oh, Michael," Peyton said on a sob, her words barely audible.

"I killed the man with my bare hands that night."

Chapter Thirteen

Heart pounding like an out of control jackhammer, Peyton leaned against the headboard, her hands hovering over her mouth. She hadn't been sure what Michael would say, but she hadn't expected that.

"A number of things saved my ass that night, but I'm grateful that I didn't have my off-duty service weapon on me. I know I would have used it if I'd had it." Michael continued as if he hadn't just dropped a bomb that made her heart race and her mind spin. Since he was once a cop, it wasn't like Peyton hadn't thought about the possibility that he had killed someone, but this. "The next few months were some of the worst months of my life. I was suspended without pay from work during the investigation, and Luke worked like hell to get the murder charge dropped to second-degree manslaughter."

Peyton hadn't noticed the tears streaming down her cheeks until Michael stopped speaking. She quickly swiped them away. Luke had been one of the most sought after defense attorneys in New York City before relocating to Cincinnati.

Michael sucked in a long, noisy breath and released it slowly while Peyton wiped her face with the back of her hand.

"After eight excruciating months," Michael continued, "I was sentenced to one year in prison, but Luke got the sentence reduced to no jail time, with two years of probation and community service. I haven't had a drink, a smoke, or a fight since that night."

Peyton didn't know what to say. She knew Michael was no angel. He wore the confident, no fear, bad-boy vibe like a badge of honor, but this...

"Peyton, I have never put my hands on a woman to cause pain. While in school, I had plenty of fights. It was clear early on that I had a problem handling situations where girls were being harassed by punk-ass boys who couldn't keep their hands to themselves. Carlton got me into therapy. It helped, but not a day goes by that I don't fear that I might be wired like Lewis."

So much made sense now. Michael's apprehension about commitment, the no drinking, the way he hovered over her when they were out and about. He feared that he was like his forefathers, internalizing what they had done and now didn't want to risk being like them.

Michael dropped back down into the chair. With the dimmed lights and her tired eyes, Peyton couldn't completely make out his features.

She climbed out of the bed and quickly grabbed her short robe from her small travel bag before slipping into it. Padding barefoot over to Michael, her steps silent on the soft, plush carpet, she had no idea what to say. Instead of speaking, Peyton sat on his lap and wrapped her arms around him, holding him tight and hoping he could feel how much she cared about him.

Michael's arms went around her waist, and he buried

his face in the crook of her neck. Her throat tightened, and goosebumps raked over her flesh. Peyton felt him. She felt the pain he relived from the situation with his father. She felt his anguish for accidentally killing a man, and she felt his relief in sharing his story.

"I'm so sorry you had to go through all of that," Peyton said close to his ear, fighting back tears. She couldn't imagine growing up fearing that her father would beat her mother or siblings. No child or anyone for that matter should have to experience that. Hearing Michael's story made her appreciate the Jenkins clan all the more.

Michael said nothing as they continued to hold each other. So many thoughts scurried through Peyton's mind. She had completely fallen for him before hearing his story, and now she didn't want to be anywhere he wasn't. And that was a problem. He made it clear, more than once, that he wasn't looking for anything serious. She got that, especially now that she better understood the reasons behind his fears. Still, that didn't stop her from wondering where this relationship could go.

Peyton placed a kiss on the side of his head before pulling back slightly. She cupped his face and stared into his beautiful eyes. *I love you* was on the tip of her tongue, but she held back. She did love him. She wasn't sure when it happened or if it was a romantic type of love. All she knew was that he made everything within her come alive. Her heart beat stronger because of him and how he made her feel.

"Michael, I…"

The lights flickered before everything went dark, except for the last of the burning embers in the fireplace. The soft background music was silenced, and Peyton no longer heard the furnace's gentle whine.

"Shit."

"Do you often get power outages?"

"It's probably just the wiring. I've been doing some renovating and have been having some electrical problems." Michael carried her to the bed and set her down. The room was pitched black, but Peyton heard him open a drawer near the bed and then there was light, a flashlight.

Peyton smiled when he flashed the light on her. "Good thing you know an electrician."

"That's right. I might be able to get some free labor out of you."

Peyton fumbled around for her tennis shoes. "Nobody said anything about free. It's after hours. My rates are tripled."

Michael laughed. "Damn, woman. I could barely afford to pay an electrician straight time, hence, the reason I'm doing the work myself. Now you want triple pay?"

"Yep. It's the middle of the night or morning depending on how you look at it. I should be sleeping, not rummaging around in the dark.

"Come on. Let's see what's going on. Maybe I can pay you in other ways."

Peyton laughed when he shone the light on his face and wiggled his eyebrows. Holding her hand, he pointed the flashlight down to light their path on the stairs.

"I'm almost afraid to ask, but what type of electrical work have you done to cause a blackout? I assume this has happened before since you didn't seem surprised when everything went dark."

"I switched out the electrical panel, and you're right, this has happened once before. I'm pretty sure I did it right, but I told myself that if the power went out again, I would hire a professional."

Sharon C. Cooper

"So that's why you invited me over, huh?" she joked. Peyton was glad she was there. Granted they still needed to talk, but her feelings for him hadn't changed. She cared more about him than she wanted to admit, especially since they hadn't known each other long.

"Peyton, I know we should have talked, really talked, before making love. I guess I just didn't want to relive that part of my life, but I needed you to know who you were dealing with. I needed you to know what type of person I am and why I avoid serious relationships. I'm still not sure if I can do this, do us."

He set the large flashlight down, the light illuminating the ceiling of the basement providing enough light to see him better, as well as the small room they were standing in.

Michael wrapped his arms around her, holding her close to his body and stared down into her face. "I care about you, but it's too soon for me to know if I can give you what you want, what you deserve."

Peyton nodded. She understood his reasons for holding back. "My feelings for you haven't changed, Michael. I like you. A lot. Though I haven't been the best judge of character when it comes to men, you don't scare me."

He gave a sputtered laughed. "Baby, I'm not trying to scare you."

"What I mean is, I'm not afraid to be with you. In my heart, I know you won't hurt me. I understand you have concerns, thinking that your father and grandfather being wife-beaters somehow spilled onto you. I get that, but you haven't given me any reason to believe that you're a detriment to my well-being." He might have the ability to break her heart, but Peyton knew he would never raise a hand to hit her.

"That means a lot to me."

"Besides, you once mentioned that other than Carlton, Luke knew you better than anyone. If that's the case, there is no way my brother-in-law would have allowed us to share a room in Jamaica. He believes in you and your character. So do I."

"Thank you." He kissed her lips.

"So is the black out and this secluded space down here all a part of your seduction plan for me?"

Michael laughed and released her. "I wish. Even I'm not this good, but if it's working for you, then yes. This was all a part of my plan."

Peyton shook her head and smiled. They were good together even if their individual insecurities were hanging over their heads.

"Alright, let's see what we have here." She opened the electrical panel, and the first thing she noticed was that none of the breakers were labeled. Then she pulled off the front cover and puffed out a breath. "Michael, what in the world...nothing in here is to code."

"So, I guess that means I didn't do it right."

"Not only is it all wrong, but you're also lucky you haven't started a fire. And why aren't any of the breakers labeled?"

"Haven't gotten that far yet."

"Are you kidding me? Do you have any idea of how long this is going to take to straighten out? I have to determine what's wired to what with the way this is set up. From now on, let's agree that you won't touch anything that involves electricity. And I guess it's safe to say that you didn't have this inspected because there's no way an inspector would have signed off on this mess."

Michael blew out a long breath and leaned against the wall next to the electrical panel. "Can you just get the lights on and fuss at me later?"

Peyton turned the flashlight on him, daring him to say something else. Returning her attention back to the panel, she shook her head. So often she saw hack jobs like what she was looking at now that were a fire waiting to happen.

"With a home this size, you might want to consider having a separate hundred-amp panel for the top floor." She moved the flashlight, illuminating the area above the panel. "Whoever installed those new pipes up there should have considered moving them someplace else. If either of those pipes leak, you're going to have a serious problem with water getting into this panel."

Michael walked up behind her and wrapped his arms around her waist. "So what is your expertise going to cost me?" he asked, nuzzling her neck and grinding against her butt, his large hands burning a path down the side of her body.

"You can't afford me." She barely got the words out before one of his hands slipped inside of her robe and cupped her breast. Stroking. Teasing. Squeezing. Peyton whimpered when he tweaked her nipple. A frisson of heat raced through her body, and the flashlight slipped from her fingers and tumbled to the concrete floor.

"You sure we can't work out a payment plan?"

Peyton moaned and leaned into him, soaking up his warmth as desire consumed her body.

"Okay. Okay, maybe we can work something out."

Chapter Fourteen

Ten long days since seeing Michael and Peyton was suffering from withdrawal. Sure they might have only known each other for just over a month, but they had a connection. A connection like nothing she had ever experienced. Peyton told herself that she could do the "friend" thing, but who was she kidding? The long distance was killing her.

She pulled a tray of chocolate chip cookies from the oven and placed them on the cooling rack. Baking and watching television had become a part of her life since returning from New York. Five amazing days with him weren't nearly enough. She wanted more.

Peyton moaned after biting into a cookie. "Definitely worth the wait," she said into the quietness of her kitchen. She had spent more time preparing meals and baking in the past couple of weeks than she had over the last three years. Her original plan after leaving New York was to head to Vegas, then on to Los Angeles. That was before she had the pleasure of getting to know Michael better. Traveling around the country alone after leaving

New York wasn't as appealing.

Peyton leaned on the kitchen counter and stared out into her backyard. She had one week left before she needed to head back to work. She spent the last couple of days thinking about her future. She loved her family and was totally committed to Jenkins & Sons Construction, but having this time off gave her an opportunity to think. She couldn't go back to working twenty hour days. That hectic schedule would send anyone to an early grave.

Michael's handsome face and sexy grin flashed across her mind. They usually talked twice a day, but it didn't seem like enough especially since Peyton could envision a future with him. She was in love. Well, at least she believed she loved Michael.

Peyton pushed away from the counter and placed the remaining cookies in a container. Still, she didn't trust her own judgment when it came to men. Three or four times of picking the wrong man had to be proof that she wasn't a good judge of character where they were concerned. Her poor choices started in high school and ended with her loser ex-husband. Dylan was her ultimate failure.

Her cell phone rang, and she hurried to the kitchen table to get it. An unexpected warmth started in her cheeks and spread through her body when Michael's name showed on the screen.

"I was just thinking about you," Peyton said when she answered.

"I've been thinking about you too," his deep sexy voice sent a shiver through her body. She would never get used to that voice, or him for that matter. Now if she could just see him face to face rather than talking on the phone, she would be crazy happy.

"How are you?"

"I'd be better if you were here spending the day with

me. I miss you."

Peyton couldn't stop the smile from spreading across her mouth. "I miss you too. I know you said that you were coming here Memorial Day weekend, but maybe you should think about moving the date up."

When he didn't respond, she feared she'd played her hand too quick. She wanted him to know that he was on her mind, but she wasn't ready to reveal just how much. Neediness wasn't a good look.

"I think you're right," Michael finally said surprising her. "I'll look into some dates and get back to you."

"That sounds great."

"So what have you been up to today?"

"Baking cookies…and thinking."

"Thinking about what?"

"Everything. Work, my life, and I've been thinking about this house." She glanced around the large, open floorplan. The four bedroom, three-bathroom home was too big for one person.

"What's going on with the house?"

"I'm thinking about selling it."

"Really? Why? I thought you loved the place."

"It's a beautiful home, but it's too big, and there are too many memories. Not all good memories."

"Why didn't you sell it right after your divorce?"

She shrugged as if he could see her and strolled into the great room, dropping down on the oversized sofa. "I wasn't ready. Letting go of the past has been hard, despite the circumstances." She didn't tell him that the house had once represented what she'd always wanted. A home with a loving husband and children running around.

An ache stabbed her in the chest remembering how much research they had done during their house hunt. The Kenwood neighborhood was perfect for raising a family and that had been the plan when she and Dylan purchased the house. Each time she thought about how she had wasted five years of her life with him, she got angry all over again.

"Peyton. Peyton?"

"I'm sorry, what?" She shook her head trying to free thoughts of her ex from her mind.

"I was asking, what's the plan after you sell the house? Where would you live?"

"I haven't thought that far ahead." She knew what she wanted. She wanted him in her future, but no way was she going to tell him. It was way too early to profess any feelings although she knew in her heart that he was the one for her. She loved the way he was with his daughter and how much he loved his mother. For some people, a generational curse was real, but in Michael's case, she felt his fears were unwarranted.

Her doorbell rang. She pushed off the sofa and went to the door, groaning when she looked out and saw Dylan standing on her stoop.

"Michael, hold on." She lowered the phone to her side and swung the door open. "Dylan, what are you doing here?" She had seen him a few months ago walking with a woman, who she'd heard he was engaged to. He still looked the same. His hair was cut close to his head, and his face, the color of mocha was as handsome as she remembered. His mustache and goatee were perfectly trimmed, and he was immaculately dressed, as usual. Her gaze went back to his eyes.

"Can we talk?"

Peyton stared at him wondering what in the world they had to talk about. She put the phone back to her ear. "Michael, can I call you back?"

"I heard you say, Dylan. What the hell is he doing

there?" She heard the edge in his voice. "Are you okay?"

"I'm fine, Babe. Let me call you right back."

"Wait!" he yelled, but Peyton disconnected anyway. He'd have more questions than she had answers. One thing she knew about Michael is that he was way too overprotective.

"What do you want, Dylan?" She stepped outside.

His gaze traveled the length of her body, reminding her that she was still dressed in her cleaning clothes, an old fitted T-shirt, worn jeans and house shoes. Her hair was pulled into a messy ponytail, and she hadn't bothered to put on any makeup since she had no plans to leave the house.

"You look good, Peyton."

"Thanks. Now why are you here?"

Her cell phone rang, and she held it up to see who was calling. *Michael.*

"Did you like the flowers I sent you a few weeks ago?" Dylan asked regaining her attention. "You used to love yellow roses."

"I used to love a lot of things," she said without missing a beat, "but my taste has changed. So is that why you've been calling me for the past few weeks? So you could find out what I thought of the flowers?"

He sighed loudly and shoved his hands into the front pockets of his dress pants. He was dressy for a Saturday afternoon, wearing a dark suit, striped oxford shirt with a bold print tie and a nice pair of black leather shoes.

"So who's Michael?"

"None of your business."

He stared at her for a moment before speaking. "I've missed you."

She let out a humorless laugh. "You gotta be kiddin' me. That's the excuse you're using to just up and stop by?

We haven't spoken in forever and all of sudden now you're calling, telling me how much you miss me?"

"I know. We were once good friends, and I should have stayed in touch. I'm sorry for everything I put you through. I just wanted to tell you that...that I'm sorry. I know you hate me, and you have every right to. What I did was unforgivable, but I'm hoping you have forgiven me."

Peyton shoved her cell phone into the back pocket of her jeans when it rang again. "What does your fiancée think about all of this?"

The surprise on his face was comical. Peyton didn't know what he was up to, but she wasn't buying that all he wanted was forgiveness.

"We broke things off a few months ago."

"Why?"

His left eyebrow rose. No doubt he was shocked she was questioning him. There was a time she took his word for everything and didn't ask many questions. Those days were gone. She learned the hard way the importance of asking questions, especially when her mind screamed that something wasn't right.

"She said that I wasn't over you." He glanced away, seeming to debate with himself of how much to say before he returned his attention to her. "I do care about her, but I'm still in love with you, PJ."

Her mouth dropped open, but she quickly recovered. "You don't cheat on someone you love!" she spat, anger roaring through her body. If only she had something to throw at his head.

"You do when you're not thinking straight. PJ, honey, I am sor—"

"Get off my property!" She said through gritted teeth. Everything she felt the night she caught him with his assistant came rushing back. Anger, disgust and hurt all rolled into one. "And stop calling me!"

He stepped forward and she took a step back, bumping into the door.

"Come on, PJ. Be reasonable. I know I messed up, but I'd hoped we could move…"

They both turned when a dark Lexus pulled into her driveway. She knew, immediately, that it was Luke's car before he opened the door. What she didn't expect was for her brother to step out of the passenger side.

"What are you guys doing here?" She said looking from one to the other.

Jerry glared at Dylan. Her brother had threatened Dylan the day after learning of his infidelity, promising to kick his ass if he ever came near her again.

"Jay, don't." Peyton jumped in front of her brother when he moved toward Dylan. Jerry was over six feet tall and had at least fifty pounds on her. Standing between them was probably not a good idea.

"Are you okay?" Luke asked her.

"I'm fine" She pushed against her brother's firm chest, backing him up to ensure he didn't do anything stupid. "Why are you two here?"

"Mike called," Luke explained as if that answered everything.

Peyton rolled her eyes.

"Why is he here?" her brother asked jabbing his finger toward Dylan. "I know you didn't invite his cheating ass over here."

Another car with dark windows screeched into her driveway, and Craig stepped out.

"Oh, this just keeps getting better." Peyton threw up her hands. "Dylan was just leaving, weren't you?" she said to her ex-husband.

"We need to talk," he said, clearly not realizing his life was in danger.

"We have nothing to talk about. I think you better leave."

"Peyton, I—"

"She said leave! Or would you prefer I throw your ass out of here?" Jerry lunged, and Craig grabbed him by the shoulder and pulled him back. Peyton didn't know who had called Craig, but having a police detective in the family had served them well on more than one occasion. Right now, her brother looked as if he wanted to kill Dylan.

"It's time for you to go," Craig said to Dylan, the authority in his voice had Peyton standing straighter. Craig had a short fuse when it came to nonsense like this.

"Dylan, just go," Peyton pleaded.

He started to speak, but with the tension bouncing off of the men in her life, he thought better of it, scurried down the walkway and climbed into his car before driving away.

Peyton glanced around at the nearby homes and didn't miss some of the curtains moving. How long had her nosy neighbors, Mrs. Hill and Mrs. Barber been standing out in their yards?

Peyton turned to Craig, Jerry, and Luke, pissed they'd come over like a bunch of thugs. No doubt Michael had sent them since she wasn't answering his calls. Apparently she needed to remind them that she could take care of herself.

"Inside, now!"

*

Michael paced the length of his office, getting more agitated by the minute. Peyton had disconnected the call before giving him a chance to tell her to keep him on the phone until after her ex-husband left. He didn't know what was going on, but she sounded different when she came back to the phone. After she had hung up, he'd called back, but got her voicemail. That's when he called Luke. If he couldn't be there for her, he was glad he had connections in the area.

"Man, you're going to wear a hole in that rug," Michael's middle brother, Bailey, said from the doorway. An Information Technology Specialist, Bailey was on his lunch break and had stopped by to fix Michaela's computer. "I'm sure you're overreacting. If she had a problem, she probably wouldn't hesitate to dial 911."

"Yeah, maybe."

Michael continued to pace. Peyton had his heart. If anything happened to her…

Bailey walked into the office, sat on the sofa and crossed his legs as if he had all the time in the world. "So Michaela was right."

"Right about what?"

"Right about Peyton being your princess. She compared you two to her favorite fairytale, *Sleeping Beauty.*

Michael stared at his brother and then laughed. "That little girl is too observant for her own good."

"So it's true."

"Sorta."

"Sorta nothing. Your ass is in love with this woman. I knew it!" He leaped from his seat. "There is no way you would have brought a woman home otherwise."

It was true that Michael had never brought a woman to his home or around Michaela. But love might be too strong of a word to describe what he felt for Peyton.

His cell phone rang, and Michael snatched it up when he saw that it was Luke.

"Where is she? Is she okay?"

"Man, she's fine. She's currently reading her brother the riot act for getting in that chump's face. Had I known Jerry would get all worked up, I wouldn't have told him what was going on. We were playing basketball when you called."

Michael sat on the edge of his desk, rubbing his forehead, glad his brother had left the room. Michael hadn't been that worked up in a long time. "Why was the ex-husband even there?" he asked Luke.

"I don't know. You have to ask PJ that. They were standing outside when we pulled up."

"Good. At least she had sense enough not to let him in the house."

"She wasn't thrilled to see us, Mike. She insisted that she could take care of herself and didn't need any of us playing hero." Luke grew quiet. "Wait. Has he done something to her? Is that why you called in a panic?"

"He's been calling her," Michael huffed. Ex-husbands didn't come around unless they wanted something and Michael had every intention of finding out what the hell this guy wanted. "What did she say about him?"

"She didn't say anything, except to stay out of her business. Oh, and as a heads up, she's still pissed. She doesn't jump to conclusions like the rest of the Jenkins' girls, but she's ridiculously independent. She's ticked that you butted in. So consider yourself warned."

"Duly noted. I can handle Peyton."

Luke laughed. "Yeah, you keep telling yourself that. Me, Craig, Zack *and* Paul thought we could handle our women too, but... Anyway, I'll let you find out for yourself. Maybe things will go differently for you, but I doubt it." Luke laughed again and told Michael that he would have Peyton call him.

Fifteen minutes later, Michael's cell phone rang.

"Hello."

"Why would you send Luke over here?" Peyton spat out and Michael straightened in his seat surprised at the venom in her voice.

"Because I was worried dammit! How you gon' just hang up on me when old boy shows up? I didn't know what the hell to think so I called Luke to go over and check on you."

"Mike, I told you I was going to call you back. That should've been enough. You wanted to know why Dylan was here, but I didn't know yet, and you didn't give me a chance to find out."

"So you're telling me the whole time he was there, he didn't tell you what he wanted? Why was he there?"

She hesitated for a second too long and every nerve in Michael's body tightened. He didn't have any claims on Peyton, but he cared too much about her to let some punk continue harassing her.

"He told me he missed me and wanted my forgiveness for the pain he caused."

Michael dropped back against his seat. He didn't know what he expected her to say, but it wasn't that. He also didn't know why he was tripping so hard. She was just a friend … a good friend. He closed his eyes and cursed under his breath. Who was he kidding? She was way more than a friend to him. She was special. And the little he knew about her ex, he knew enough to know she was too damn good for him. Hell, she was too good for him too, but still…

"What did you tell him?" Michael finally asked, hearing the edge in his own voice. "Do you forgive him? Do you miss him?"

"I forgive him, but I didn't tell him that. I didn't get a chance to tell him much of anything because my brother showed up with Luke, ready to put a beating on Dylan."

Good, Michael wanted to say but didn't. No need to fuel an already volatile conversation. He didn't know Dylan, but he wanted to get his hands on the guy for breaking Peyton's heart.

"So tell me, Peyton. Why are you so pissed about Luke and Jerry showing up?"

"Because I can take care of myself. They embarrassed me, acting like I'm some helpless female when the situation didn't warrant them being here, Michael. Had you not called them, we wouldn't be having this conversation."

"Peyton, I have no doubt you can take care of yourself, but when you abruptly hung up on me, I didn't know what to think. I did the first thing that came to mind, and that was to call for back up. I'm sorry if you were embarrassed or if I overstepped, but I did what I had to do." And he would do it again.

Peyton huffed out a breath. "Okay, I can see we're getting nowhere with this discussion. I don't want to argue with you."

"Hmm, our first argument as a…" He started to say as a couple, but they weren't a couple, thanks to him.

"Michael, you and I are friends. I get it. I respect your reasons for not wanting more, but with that, you have to understand that you don't get a say in anything I do, or anyone I talk to. Yes, Dylan hurt me and yes every time I hear his voice or see him I have flashbacks of when I walked in on him and his assistant, but I survived. So until I'm your woman, stay out of my personal affairs."

Michael stared at the phone when she disconnected.

"Damn. She is mad."

Chapter Fifteen

"I had a nice time today," Landen said to Peyton, dividing his attention between her and the road. He steered his BMW into her neighborhood and slammed on the brakes when a boy on a blue dirt bike dashed across the street. Now that the weather was a little warmer, children were outside running across neighbors lawns and playing in the street. "I would love to take you out again. Can I call you sometime?"

Peyton hesitated. Toni had set her up on the blind date insisting she needed to jump start Peyton's social life. Landen, a COO for a mid-level tech company, was a nice guy, but there were no sparks. Peyton hated comparing him to Michael, but that's exactly what she did the whole time they were together. The men were opposites in every way, from the type of work they did to the way they dressed. Where Michael was cocky and laid-back, Landen was geeky and straight-laced and no longer her type.

Instead of turning Landen down outright, she said, "You can call me, but I have to warn you. I go back to work in a few days, and I'm sure I'll have some serious catching up to do."

"I know what that's like." He pushed his wire-rimmed glasses up on his nose. "We can play it by ear."

Landen turned onto Peyton's street and stopped for Mrs. Hill, who was backing out of her driveway. Seconds later, he pulled into Peyton's driveway, and her heart did a somersault when she spotted the lone figure standing on her stoop.

Michael.

She tried to play it cool, but the butterflies in her stomach went crazy, fluttering around like wild birds. It was as if thoughts of him had conjured him up.

"A friend of yours?" Landen asked.

"Uh, yeah. I didn't know he was stopping by." That was an understatement. She wasn't expecting him for another two weeks, Memorial Day weekend. Frustrated with the long distance between them and still a little peeved about him sending Luke and Jerry to her house three days ago, she'd kept the telephone conversations with Michael brief. Talking to him only made her miss him that much more and she was tired of torturing herself.

Landen parked in front of the two-car garage and before she could stop him, he exited the vehicle and opened her car door. After the way Michael reacted about Dylan, Peyton decided to say goodbye to her date at the car.

"Landen, thanks so much for a very nice afternoon."

"It was great meeting you, Peyton. I look forward to us doing this again sometime." He waved his hand toward her front stoop. "Can I walk you to the door?"

Michael stood in the walkway, his arms folded across his chest. He looked so dangerously handsome that Peyton wondered if something was wrong with her for falling for someone like him. A man who had no fear and did whatever the hell he wanted.

"That's not necessary, Landen. Thanks again. It was nice spending time with you."

"Same here." He bent down and kissed her cheek. He was an old school gentleman. Her grandmother would love him.

Peyton watched as her date pulled out of the driveway. Her heart did a giddy up when she turned, and her gaze met Michael's. Still standing in the same spot, he didn't look too pleased. What was she going to do with him?

"Well this is a surprise," she said, the breathiness of her tone betraying the coolness she wanted to portray. He looked delicious. The gray T-shirt molded against his muscular upper body and his black jeans hung low on his hips, the pant legs sticking partially out of a pair of black Timberland boots. "What are you doing here?" She stopped in front of him. She lifted her hand and cupped his cheek, his five o'clock shadow tickling her palm. Peyton loved this look on him.

Michael still didn't speak. His gaze bore into her with those light-brown eyes that she dreamed about every night. He turned his head and placed a kiss in her palm, still not speaking. Instead, he pulled her against his hard body. His expert lips touched hers, and every cell within Peyton came alive.

Peyton dropped her handbag, unfazed by the thunk the purse made when it hit the concrete. Her arms went around his neck, and she held on to the man she loved. He was the one she wanted. No one else.

"I've missed you so damn much." The huskiness in his sexy voice held so much emotion. She was glad that he had been just as affected by the distance between them. "I don't like it when we argue."

Peyton leaned back and smiled. "It's only been one argument."

"I know, and I didn't like it."

"Me either. Let's go inside and you can tell me what you're doing here."

＊

Michael grabbed an overnight bag from the trunk of the rental car and followed her inside. Just as he expected, the inside of Peyton's home was just as pristine as the manicured lawn.

"Nice place." He set his bag just inside the door and strolled farther into the house. The light colored walls, sparkling hardwood floors, and white furniture made it clear that she didn't have children running around.

"Thanks." Peyton turned on lights now that the sun was setting. She closed the blinds, telling him to make himself at home.

"So who was the guy in the Beemer?" He asked, leaning against a nearby wall, his legs crossed at the ankle. It took all of his willpower to stay put when the guy helped her out of the car and then kissed her. Michael knew that if he had approached her at that moment, he would have lost her for sure. He had already feared that he'd blown his shot with her.

Peyton turned to him, her gaze taking him in. He loved it when she looked at him the way she was now as if she wanted to rip his clothes off. But seeing some other man kiss her, even on the cheek, had his blood boiling.

"My date," she said. She walked into the kitchen without elaborating and pulled a bottle of water from the refrigerator. "Do you want something to drink? Are you hungry?"

He pushed away from the wall, searching his mind to choose his next words carefully. "I didn't realize you were dating."

"I wasn't. Not until Toni told me that I needed a social life and set me up on a blind date."

Michael cursed under his breath. "How long have you been seeing him?"

She took a swig from her drink. "Not long."

"Dammit, Peyton. What the hell? I thought we had something here. So what was up with you saying that you missed me every time I called? You playin' me?"

Peyton's brows drew together, and she set the water bottle down on the counter. She approached him, her eyes narrowed. She had the same expression on her face the day he first met her, the day he had offered her two hundred dollars for her airplane seat.

"Michael, you're the one who told me you weren't relationship material. You're the one who called us 'friends.' And you're the one who doesn't want a commitment." She jabbed a finger in his chest. "So don't come to my house expecting to get something you're not willing to give! I'm thirty-five years old, and I'm ready for the next chapter in my life. That includes marriage and hopefully children."

"Peyton, I'm—"

"Yes, I've missed you. My heart aches every time you call. I can't stare into your beautiful eyes when you talk to me on the telephone. I can't get all hot and bothered when you touch me because you're not touching me when we're on the telephone." Tears swelled in her eyes, hitting him like a steal beam to the head. He never wanted to be the cause of a woman's tears, especially one that meant as much to him as Peyton. "I can't keep going like this with you."

Panic lodged in Michael's throat, and he struggled to swallow. It had taken him a lifetime to find her. He couldn't lose her now. Not like this. Not because he was afraid of one day hurting her.

He was torn on how to deal with his inability to see into the future and know for sure whether or not he'd be just like his father and grandfather. Was he willing to take the chance? Was he willing to risk Peyton's life or his own? He didn't know what scared him the most, being in a committed relationship or losing her.

"I can't keep longing for you from afar," Peyton continued. "If you don't want more than a friendship with me, that's fine. But don't you dare come here and question me about going out with someone who does. I care about you. You mean so much to me, but you're crazy if you think I'm going to sit around forever and wait for you."

He stared at her, and his heart swelled. The emotion in her voice and the sadness in her eyes pummeled his insides.

He stepped to her and cupped her face in his hands. "You're right, I am crazy. I'm crazy in love with you. Baby, I don't want to lose you. Whatever I need to do to prove that to you, consider it done."

He didn't give her a chance to speak. His mouth covered hers as he kissed her with everything he had in him, hoping she could feel how much he loved her. *Home.* That's what it felt like having her in his arms. He meant what he said. He would do whatever it took to prove to her that he was ready for a commitment.

With one last peck on the lips, he dropped his hands, giving them both a chance to catch their breath. She didn't move, her gaze steadied on him until a small smile touched her kiss-swollen lips.

"What?"

"You said you loved me." Her voice was airy, a slight

tint to her cheeks.

"I know." Saying the words out loud hadn't been as hard as he thought they would be.

"You do know that means you're stuck with me, right? No take backs."

He laughed, shaking his head. Some of the tension clawing through his body only minutes ago dissipated.

He reached for her hand and brought her fingers to his lips. "I can think of worse things to be stuck with."

The smile on her face could light up the darkest night. Luke might have been right. Peyton was good for him. She was definitely what he needed, what he wanted.

"I love you too." Peyton wrapped her arms around his neck, and his went automatically around her waist. She felt so good in his arms. "I've missed you so much."

"The last few days of not talking to you longer than a minute made me nuts. I couldn't wait until the end of the month. I needed to see you today. I needed to hold you." He placed a lingering kiss against the side of her head, breathing in her fresh scent. This was where she was supposed to be, in his arms.

Michael leaned back and did something he wanted to do from the moment he saw her in the driveway. He pulled out the pins holding her bun in place and set them on the nearby counter. Fluffing her hair, he tugged slightly, forcing her head back so he could look into her eyes.

"That's better."

"I agree." She lifted her hands to his face, warmth traveling through his body. "Have I ever told you that I like this look on you?" She rubbed the hair on his cheek.

"You might have mentioned it a time or two."

"It fits this bad-boy image you have going on."

He chuckled. Of course, Miss Prim and Proper would

like his look whereas others saw him and assumed he was a troublemaker. The rugged appearance played well when he took on certain types of cases, like the one he started four days ago. Some skittish informants were more willing to share information with him when he wasn't clean shaven.

"So what does the rest of your evening look like?" Michael asked.

"Well," she ran her hands down his chest and farther down to his belt buckle, "I thought that maybe I could show you my bedroom, and we could get reacquainted."

"Mmm, I love the way you think, Boss Lady." Michael bent slightly, palmed the back of her thighs, and lifted her. A squeal slipped through her lips. She wrapped her arms and legs around him and held on tight. He couldn't wait to get reacquainted.

Chapter Sixteen

"Are you still going to my grandparents' house with me tomorrow for Sunday Brunch?" Peyton pulled the pork tenderloin and roasted potatoes out of the oven and set the dish on the stove top. She and Michael had established a comfortable routine since his arrival two days ago. They'd spent that time touring Cincinnati, dining at some of her favorite eateries like, Skyline Chili and lounging around the house. "Michael," she said when she realized he hadn't responded.

"Baby, I'm going wherever you go," he said absently. He'd been sitting at the kitchen table working on his laptop and sending texts back and forth to his assistant for the past forty-five minutes. No way was she going to complain, though. She was glad he was there. "You guys do brunch every Sunday?" he asked.

"Yep, every week. Rarely do any of us miss a Sunday brunch and if we do, it's because we're out of town. And if we're not out of town and don't show, we can expect to hear from my grandmother Monday morning."

Michael nodded.

An anxious flutter scurried through her stomach. Peyton hadn't invited a man to Sunday brunch in a long time. Michael attending with her would be like announcing to the family that she was serious about this man.

*

Michael closed his laptop and set it aside. He had to tell Peyton that he'd been doing some digging into her ex-husband's life, but he worried about how she would take the news. The day Dylan had shown up on her doorstep, Michael's protective instincts kicked in with a vengeance. Initially, he hadn't found much, but he found enough to make him dig deeper.

"What's on your mind?" Peyton set a plate in front of him. Her cooking skills were second to none, one of many things he was learning about her.

Michael inhaled the delicious aroma. His mouth watered at the sight of the pork tenderloin. A meat and potatoes kind of guy, he appreciated the way she indulged his healthy appetite in more ways than just food.

"Michael?"

He lifted his head. "Yeah, babe?"

"What's going on? What's on your mind?"

After a slight hesitation, he stood and pulled out the chair next to him. "Have a seat." He slid her plate in front of her. "There's something I need to talk to you about."

Concern covered her beautiful face. "What's wrong? Are we—"

"We're fine." He held her hand, surprised that it was freezing. He squeezed it, hoping to reassure her that everything between them was okay. "It's about Dylan."

Her brows furrowed. "What about him?"

"Don't be mad, but I've been doing a little investigating."

"Michael." Peyton slammed back against the chair. "I told you. There is nothing between Dylan and me. You have nothing to worry about. You're the only man I want."

He chuckled and kissed her. "I'm glad because I wouldn't want to have to take some dude out for stepping to you."

"That's not funny."

"Okay. You're right. Not funny."

"So why are you looking into Dylan? He's not a part of my life."

"I know. But it was bothering me that he kept calling you and then showed up here. Based on my experience, an ex-husband doesn't do that after three years of no contact unless he wants something." Michael wasn't sure if Dylan wanted Peyton back or was after something she had. Either way, her ex-husband was in for a rude awakening if he thought he was getting her back.

Peyton shook her head. "I don't want to know. Whatever is going on with Dylan, is none of my business. He and I are done. He can fall off the face of the earth, and I would be okay not knowing. So whatever you found, keep it to yourself."

Michael continued debating with himself. In his line of work, anything that stood out and seemed unusual often pointed to a problem. He could leave Peyton in the dark since what he found so far wasn't much, but it was enough to raise suspicion.

After saying a quick prayer over the meal, Peyton picked up her fork and stabbed it into a potato.

"Dylan has a million-dollar life insurance policy out on you."

Peyton's hand stalled, the fork halfway to her mouth. She didn't speak as she lowered it to the plate. "Why?"

Michael shook his head and grabbed hold of her hand again. "I don't know, baby, but I plan to find out. In the meantime, stay away from him. This could be nothing, but it could also be something. I don't want you going anywhere by yourself. Okay?"

She nodded, and he squeezed her thigh under the table.

"It looks as if Dylan had the policy while you guys were married, but raised the amount six months ago."

"How is that possible? Wouldn't the insurance company require me to take a physical or something?"

"For that amount, probably, but if you know the right people," Michael shrugged, "you can do just about anything."

Peyton picked at her food. Michael didn't regret telling her that part. She needed to be aware of her surroundings.

"Have you told anyone else that you were looking into Dylan's life?"

"No, only you."

"Good. I don't want my family to know."

"Peyton."

"Michael, my family knows enough about my personal life. I just want to keep this between you and me. Besides, Dylan has done some crappy things, but I don't think he would do anything to physically hurt me."

"That might be so, but I'm not willing to take that chance."

"You think he wants to kill me?"

Michael hesitated. "I'm not sure. It wouldn't be the first time some asshole tried to collect on a spouse, or an ex-spouse."

Peyton's brows drew together, and she opened her mouth but pursed her lips without saying what was on her mind.

"Listen, I'll be here until Tuesday. I know you're planning to go back to work Monday, and you should be fine there. As for getting around the city, we can have someone drive you around. Or I can make some calls and assign someone to you."

"You're not serious? Don't you think that's going to raise suspicion with my family?"

He glared at her, tempted to tell her that as long as she was safe, he didn't give a damn if her family knew that something wasn't right with Dylan. Instead, he said, "Forget having a driver. If it makes you feel better, I'll just have someone watching your back."

Peyton stared at him. Michael had no clue what was going on in that pretty little head of hers. He expected some pushback, but so far, the conversation was going better than he expected.

They ate in silence until Peyton reiterated that she didn't want her family to know about Dylan. Michael agreed to keep quiet unless Dylan started coming around again.

*

Peyton barely tasted her food as she finished off her vegetables. There was no way Dylan had intentions of getting rid of her to cash in the life insurance policy. Even he wasn't stupid enough to think he could get away with something like that.

She thought back on their brief conversations over the last few weeks. He told her that he wanted to talk about something important. Was he in some type of trouble?

"Last night, you know how you talked more about selling your house," Michael interrupted her thoughts, "and saying that you didn't want to go back to work just yet?"

Peyton nodded, twisting the fork handle back and forth, not caring that the utensil clanged against the plate. A month off work should have been long enough to figure out what she wanted to do with her life. It hadn't been. All she knew at the moment was that she wanted to take off a couple of more weeks and think about her future.

"I want you to come back to New York with me."

Peyton turned her head to Michael so fast it felt as if she had pulled a muscle in her neck. "What? What are you saying?"

"I'm saying I don't want to do a long distance relationship if we don't have to. Why not come home with me, spend some time thinking about what you want. You don't have to worry about a place to stay, food or anything. I got you."

"What you mean is that you want to keep an eye on me and make sure Dylan can't find me." Peyton stood with her plate and strolled over to the sink, putting some distance between her and Michael.

"Baby, it's not like that." He walked up behind her, pulling her against his body. "Yes, I'm concerned about your well-being, especially since I can't get a read on what your ex is up to. But that's not the only reason I want you to go home with me."

He turned her around, and she studied his face, trying to keep an open mind regarding his request.

"I want us to get to know each other better, spend more time together. Since you have more flexibility than me, I thought maybe you can consider extending your leave. You can hang out in New York with my family and me for a couple of weeks, or longer if you want."

His offer was appealing on many levels. Thinking about her family and the business gave her pause, but she'd been considering making changes in her life. She had enough money to live off on comfortably for years, so her finances weren't an issue. Maybe it was time for something new. Something exciting. She had no doubt that any time spent with Michael would be an adventure.

She glanced up and met his gaze. "Let me think about it."

*

Michael lounged in the family room on the lower level of the Jenkins' home, sitting in one of the big leather chairs next to Luke. A minimum of twenty-five guys were scattered about in the multi-purpose room that had been divided into several sections. Some stood around the pool table talking smack, while others shot darts. Michael, Luke, Zack and Paul were sitting in the front of the big screen television watching an NBA game. L.A. was getting pummeled by Portland.

"I can't watch anymore." Zack stood. "I'm going upstairs. You guys want anything?"

The only thing Michael wanted was Peyton, but the last time he was upstairs, the women shooed him out of the kitchen. He had only gone up to check on her, or so he told himself. He knew she was safe, but every day he found out a little bit more about her ex, making Michael fear for her safety.

"So I guess you and Peyton are getting along pretty well," Luke said when Paul left them to go into the card room. The guys in there were playing Spades and every so often Michael heard yelling about someone cheating.

"We're doing good."

"How good?"

Michael turned his full attention to his friend. "Why? What have you heard?"

Luke chuckled. "I'm not saying I heard anything, but

there's something different about you today. When you stopped by my office the day you arrived in Cincinnati, you were agitated, prickly. Since you and PJ have been holed up in her house for the last few days, you should be more at ease, but you're not."

No one knew Michael the way Luke knew him. He could look at him and know what he was feeling or thinking. To keep his promise to Peyton, Michael hadn't said a word about her ex. Besides not wanting to piss Peyton off, he didn't want to cause an uproar unless he knew for sure Dylan was up to something. Although his gut told him that it was only a matter of time before Dylan showed his hand. Michael had obtained photos of Dylan and was just waiting for him to misstep.

"So what's up?" Luke broke into Michael's thoughts. "Your silence has me even more concerned."

Michael knew he could trust Luke with his life, but when the source of Michael's worry involved Peyton, he wasn't so sure Luke could be impartial. She might have been his sister-in-law, but he saw her as his sister, his family.

"Whatever you say stays right here," Luke added as if reading Michael's mind.

Michael sat forward, his elbows on his knees. "I'm worried about Peyton's safety." He didn't elaborate, but he could hear the gears churning in Luke's mind. His features hardened.

"If that's the case, her family needs to know."

Michael shook his head. "Not gonna happen. She doesn't want them involved, and I'm handling it."

Again Luke hesitated before speaking. "Well, you know where I am if you need me."

"I know. I have you on speed dial."

"I have a feeling there's more." Luke shifted in his

seat, turning toward Michael.

"I asked Peyton to return to New York with me, indefinitely.

Luke sat back, rubbing a hand along his mouth and chin. While Michael was quick to react, Luke was a thinker. His cool, calm demeanor had served him well over the years. One of the smartest men Michael knew and a damn good lawyer, Michael knew his friend would have an opinion about what he'd shared, but not before asking a ton of questions.

"What are your intentions with Peyton?"

Michael met Luke's gaze head on. "I'm in love with her. I don't know how or when it happened, but I am crazy in love with that woman." Actually, Michael knew when he fell for Peyton. He just hadn't been ready to put a name or emotion to what he felt about her at the time. It was the morning of the wedding. The day they woke up in bed together. Somehow she looked different to him that morning. There was a vulnerability, a softness to her that he hadn't noticed days earlier. Something in his heart shifted.

"I see," is all Luke said, still looking thoughtful.

"Luke, I promise you I will never do anything to hurt her."

"Not intentionally, but do you think you're ready for the type of commitment she wants?"

Michael was slow to respond. In his heart he was ready, but he'd be lying if he said that he didn't still have concerns about his issues. They had spent practically every waking moment together since he had arrived in Cincinnati, co-existing effortlessly. He just didn't know if a few days were enough to know if he was wired like his father and grandfather.

Instead of repeating his question, Luke said, "Look

around." He pointed at the men in the large open space. "If you do anything to hurt her, intentional or not, they will come looking for your ass. Peyton is the chosen one, man, for lack of a better way of explaining what she means to this family. They hold her in the same esteem as they do their grandparents. Like them, she's part of the glue that keeps the family together. They're protective of each other, but more so of Peyton."

"Oh great," Michael murmured and sat back in his seat. "No pressure here."

He glanced around the room at her family. They were a group you didn't want to screw with. But Michael also knew that he was willing to take the chance at finding happiness with Peyton. Besides, he couldn't let her go even if he wanted to. He was in too deep. His heart was in too deep.

Chapter Seventeen

"If I tell you something, do you promise not to say anything to anyone?" Peyton asked Martina. They had always been each other's confidant, and Peyton trusted her more than anyone. But what she had to tell her, would affect all of their lives.

They were the only two remaining at the dining room table, munching on what was left of the vegetable tray sitting in the middle of the long table. The oversized dining room shared a wall with one of the sitting rooms that could be considered a living room, a large arched opening provided a view of family members hanging out there.

Jada, Christina, and Toni had kitchen duty, while some of their aunts came in and out of the dining room grabbing dishes and platters of leftover food.

Martina stopped chewing, her fork dangling from her fingers and she studied Peyton. The way she narrowed her eyes, Peyton knew Martina was about to say something stupid.

"I'll promise not to say anything on three conditions."

Now Peyton was the one probably looking crazy. "Okay," she dragged out the word, afraid of what the conditions would be. With Martina, there was no telling.

"Your secret is safe with me unless you're secretly married, pregnant or paint nudes."

And there it is. Peyton shook her head and laughed. "Something is wrong with you! Why would you think any of those things would apply to me?"

"Duh, do you know the Jenkins women? There have been more surprises like those in the last two years than this family needs. Whatever you have to say cannot be more shocking than any of those."

"Good point." Peyton grabbed a small carrot from the veggie tray and dipped it in the French onion dip before taking a bite. "I'm thinking about leaving Jenkins & Sons Construction."

"What?" Martina jumped up and yelled. Everyone around stopped what they were doing to see what was going on.

Peyton propped a fake grin on her face and shook her head while pulling Martina back down into her seat.

"Would you keep your voice down?"

"Not if you're going to drop bombs like that. What are you thinking? You can't leave. You *are* Jenkins & Sons."

Peyton marinated on her cousin's words. For years Peyton had dedicated her life to the business, losing sleep and giving up her weekends. She loved being an electrician and enjoyed managing Jenkins & Sons. But, she wanted more.

"Does this have anything to do with your boy-toy?"

Peyton nodded. "He asked me to spend a few weeks, or longer in New York with him."

Martina remained silent, which was not her norm.

"Just say it MJ. Whatever is rolling around in that

convoluted brain of yours just spit it out."

"I can tell Mike loves you. He's been roaming around here all morning long with that puppy dog look in his eyes."

Peyton laughed. "Would you be serious?"

"I'm dead serious. Question is, do you love him?"

"Why do you two have your heads together over here?" Jada asked as she and Toni sat on either side of Peyton and Martina.

"You have to be the nosiest person on the planet," Martina snapped. "Why do you two insist on knowing everything about everybody?"

"That's our job," Jada said.

Peyton noticed Martina rubbing her stomach, something she'd been doing since they sat down. Her cousin hadn't complained, but looked tired, and she'd been wincing every few minutes.

"We know something's going on," Toni said, her gaze on Peyton, daring her to deny her claim. "Ever since you walked in with the cutie P.I, you've been acting different, more relaxed. So either he's been putting it on you real good these last few days, or you have a secret that you're trying to keep from all of us."

"Yeah, spill it," Jada added.

Christina walked toward them.

"Okay. So what's going on over here?" She sat in the chair next to Jada and swiped a celery stick from Martina's plate, munching on it. Peyton hadn't talked to her sister much since returning from New York and wondered how married life was treating her. If the constant smile on her face were any indication, she'd be willing to guess all was well in Christina's life.

Peyton wondered if the joy bubbling inside of her was written on her face. The last few days with Michael had been some of the best days of her life. Was Toni right? Did she look as if she'd been experiencing the best loving ever?

"MJ? What's wrong?" Peyton stood slowly, her hand on her cousin's back. Perspiration laced Martina's forehead, and her brows were pinched together as if she was going to be sick. Martina hadn't suffered from morning sickness in months, though early in her pregnancy she spent most of the days with her head over the toilet.

"I don't feel good." Martina placed her forearm on the table and laid her head on it, her other hand holding her stomach. Peyton rubbed her back until Martina jerked back in her seat, both arms around her mid-section. "Oh, shi…"

Martina struggled to stand. Water ran down the inside of her khaki color pant legs and tears spilled from her eyes.

"Oh my God." Jada leaped out of her seat along with Toni.

"Her water just broke," Toni said, stating the obvious.

"Okay, let's just stay calm," Christina said in her normal soothing voice. She and Peyton stood on each side of Martina, holding her arms at the elbow.

Martina cried out in pain and doubled over.

"Paul!" They all screamed at once, causing everyone to rush into the room, talking at once.

"Jada, find Paul. We'll meet him at his truck," Peyton instructed. Her heart pounded faster than the flapping wings of a hummingbird. Uneasiness gripped her body. Martina wasn't due to deliver for another month. "CJ, help me get her to the truck."

*

Michael's gaze followed Peyton as she paced the

length of the waiting room. Worry lines creased Peyton's beautiful forehead, her shoulders sagged as they waited for word on Martina and the baby.

Memories of the day Michaela was born rose to the surface. Though he and Octavia had agreed they were better as just friends, she wanted him in the delivery room. Watching a life being brought into this world was an experience Michael would never forget.

Until recently, he hadn't thought about having more children, but with Peyton in his life, the idea had come up more than once. He saw how she was with his daughter – loving, gentle and a push over. The last thought brought a smile to his face. She would be a wonderful addition to his family.

"Peyton," he called. She stopped, and he stretched his hand to her.

"Baby, are you trying to wear out the floor?" He pulled her against him, the gardenia scent of her hair reminding him of their shower that morning.

"It's been hours. No one has told us anything," she mumbled against his chest. He rubbed his hand up and down her back, loving how perfectly she fit in his arms.

He kissed the top of her head. "Are you hungry? We can go to the cafeteria for a while. Maybe by the time we come back, the family will know something. Besides, you could use a minute to relax. You've been wound pretty tight since we arrived."

She lifted her head. "MJ vowed years ago that she would never have children, and I guess I just want everything to go perfectly for her."

"I know. I'm sure she's fine. Besides, Paul is with her. He—"

"He's probably passed out."

Michael laughed. "You're right. He did seem a little

out of his element on the way here." Supposedly the former Senator was normally the epitome of calm, but he'd been a wreck, especially each time Martina cried out in pain. Luke ended up driving both of them to the hospital.

Peyton smiled and warmth spread through Michael. Each passing day he fell more and more in love with her. He wanted to ask whether or not she had thought more about their conversation, about her taking an indefinite leave from work and going back to New York with him. He wanted to keep her close until they figured out what Dylan was up to. More importantly, he wanted to see if they could build on what was already developing between them. Since she wasn't ready to go back to work, it seemed like the perfect solution.

He placed a lingering kiss on her lips. "So you want to go for a walk with me?"

"I want to, but I want to be here just in case there's any news. What do you think about going in search of some ice cream?"

He lifted a brow. "Ice cream?"

"Yeah, I have a taste for some."

He didn't want to deny her of anything, but he also had no intention of leaving her side.

"I'm not leaving you."

Peyton sighed. She hooked her fingers into his two front belt loops. "I know you don't want to hear this, but I think you're overreacting about Dylan. I haven't seen him since that day, and he hasn't done anything that would make me believe that he's up to no good."

Michael straightened and dropped his arm from around her. "Just because you don't think he's up to no good doesn't mean that he's not." The words came out more abrasive than he'd planned and she narrowed her eyes at him. Evidently, she didn't appreciate his response.

"Hey, I'm making a coffee run," Luke said, standing a couple of feet behind Peyton. "You guys want anything?"

"Actually, why don't you take Michael with you? He could stand to go for a walk," Peyton said.

Michael shook his head. "I'm not lea—"

"Baby, look around." Peyton squeezed his hand. "I'm not alone. and it's not like you're going to be gone that long. Go. And while you're at it, find me some ice cream. Anything but chocolate."

He stood there a second longer, his gaze skimming the small room overrun with the Jenkins family. She was right. No way would Dylan try anything with so many of them around.

He pulled her close and kissed her cheek. "Don't go anywhere without someone."

She shook her head and smiled. "You can take the man out of the police department, but not the policeman out of the man."

Michael followed Luke out of the room. He hated being over protective, but he couldn't help it. She was a part of him. The thought of possibly leaving her in Cincinnati put him even more on edge. If she decided not to go back to New York with him, he would have to come up with another plan.

"I can't believe you're worried about PJ. She's surrounded by her family," Luke said when they headed for the stairwell. "This must be more serious than you let on."

"I'm not sure yet, but I do feel better knowing she's not alone."

The Jenkins family were some of the nicest people he'd ever met, but no doubt they would step in if they sensed trouble. They were also a reminder that he and

Peyton came from two different worlds. There were many nights he and his mother prayed that Lewis wouldn't show up for dinner. Unlike Peyton's grandmother who practically sent out a search party if any of her family didn't show up for Sunday brunch.

Michael never cared what people thought, but he couldn't help wondering what the Jenkins family would say if Peyton agreed to go back to New York with him.

*

Hours later Peyton sat in Martina's hospital room holding her little goddaughter, Janay Peyton Kendricks. Peyton's heart split open in awe. The miracle of life never ceased to amaze her.

"She is absolutely perfect, MJ."

Martina gave a sleepy smile followed by a yawn. She'd been dozing on and off since she had summoned Peyton into the room.

"You're going to have to make sure you visit Cincinnati often so that you don't miss too much of your goddaughter's firsts. The first time she babbles, first steps, first word, fir—"

"Slow down, MJ." Peyton stood and placed a sleeping Janay in the bassinet-like baby bed next to Martina. "I haven't decided if I'm going to—"

"You're going. You have to. You have practically given up your life to run Jenkins & Sons. It's time you found some happiness, and I know Michael's the man for the job."

Peyton smiled. "When you first met him, you said that he was a slick talking chump, not worthy of me."

Martina waved her off. "Since when did you start listening to me? He's still a chump, but a good chump."

They both laughed, and Peyton leaned against the bed, wondering if she could move so far away from her family and Martina, her best friend. Just like the family was dependent on her, she was dependent on them. They had been her support, her rock over the last few years and she couldn't imagine not seeing at least one of them every day.

"Take it from me. When love comes knocking at your door, you have to answer. Otherwise, you might miss out on the best thing that has ever happened to you. I have to admit I had my doubts about old Mikey, but seeing the way he looks at you and the way you look at him... Well, you two are nauseating to look at."

Peyton threw her head back and laughed. That was high praise coming from Martina. She didn't go easy on many, but she hadn't given Michael as hard a time as she gave Craig, Zack, and Luke when they started dating the Jenkins' girls.

Peyton glanced down at the baby. Getting her heart broken again terrified her, but if she didn't follow her heart she would always wonder what could have been between her and Michael.

Chapter Eighteen

Peyton stood at the window of her grandfather's study, staring out at the side yard. The grounds were just as beautiful as the inside of the house because the gardens were her grandmother's pride and joy.

Peyton turned and leaned on the back of her grandfather's large, desk chair. The office had always been one of her favorite spots in the house. There was just something about the space that always brought her peace.

The door to the study swung open, grabbing Peyton's attention.

"Hey, Sweetheart. Sorry, I'm late." Steven Jenkins hurried in and set his briefcase next to the desk. He had retired years ago, but still kept himself busy meeting with old friends and consulting with other businesses. "Have you been waiting long?"

"No, not too long." She hugged him, hanging on longer than usual, soaking up the strength and love she always felt when they embraced. When they separated, he directed her to the large leather sofa. "You look nice," Peyton said.

Her grandfather removed his dark suit jacket, setting it on the arm of a nearby chair before loosening his paisley tie. He had recently started wearing suspenders, but they didn't detract from his imposing height and authoritative presence.

"I had a couple of meetings this morning, but I know you didn't stop by to talk about me. So what's going on?"

Peyton rubbed her hands together, suddenly a little nervous about talking to the patriarch of the Jenkins family. The day before, she mentioned to her cousin Nick, that she was taking more time off. She didn't give him details on why because she wanted to tell her grandfather first.

"I just wanted to let you know what my plans are for the next few weeks."

"Okay."

"When you realized dad, and everyone else wasn't ready or interested in taking over Jenkins & Sons, you trusted me with the responsibility."

Her grandfather didn't interrupt. He had always been a good listener. He was such an important person in Peyton's life, and she valued his opinion and support. Support she needed now.

"I'm extending my leave of absence." Her siblings and cousins were more than capable of running the business. "I'm going back to New York with Michael and I don't know for how long. I'm not trying to abandon the business or the family, but Michael and I have something special, and I want to explore what that something might be."

Her grandfather stretched his arm and rested it on the back of the sofa. "Peyton, I have watched you grow up to be a beautiful, successful, and intelligent woman who I am extremely proud of. The number of clients we have has multiplied, and so have profits under your leadership. Like I've often said, you're irreplaceable."

"Grampa."

"Let me finish. With all that said, I know what you've been through these last few years. After Dylan's indiscretions, you gave up your life to run the business. Though I think you're irreplaceable, and you have represented this family well, I want you to be happy. I want that more than anything else for you."

A knot twisted inside of her at her grandfather's loving words.

They both stood.

"Thank you, Grampa. I love you."

"I love you too, sweetheart," he said hugging her. "I love you very much. If you think going back to New York with this young man will make you happy, I'll support that."

Her grandfather released her and walked over to the oak desk. He picked up the small stack of mail and started sifting through the envelopes. Peyton had a feeling there was more he planned to say. She'd been in plenty of meetings with him and on the receiving end of a few of his lectures. She knew the sign. He hadn't dismissed her and was probably thinking about his next words.

She waited.

"These last few years witnessing your sister and your cousins fall for their now husbands has been interesting to watch. Katherine and I have always tried to support you girls without getting too deep into your business, but there is something we don't understand. Our children and you kids were not raised to think that shacking up is okay." He dropped the mail and returned his attention to her. "I didn't say anything to you in Jamaica because your grandmother told me not to, but I'll admit to being surprised. The others didn't surprise me as much, but you…"

Peyton tried not to fidget, but he was wearing that no-nonsense look that he usually reserved for Martina and Jada, the problem kids. This was a first for Peyton.

"I know it's not fair for me to expect more from you than I might expect from the others, but I do. You have always carried yourself with pride, and you've been such a wonderful role model to your sister and cousins."

Sadness stirred in Peyton's stomach. Since before she could remember, she had always tried to be the perfect child, the child that didn't talk back nor got into trouble. So hearing that her grandparents were disappointed in her, was a severe blow.

"Back in my day, we courted a girl, fell in love, met her parents, got married, and then we shared a bed. There was none of this sleeping or living together first. You kids have tossed—"

"Grampa, I have always had the utmost respect for you, Gramma and my parents. I've tried living up to your expectations and have tried to be the *good girl*. But for years, I didn't like myself as much as I like myself now. For the first time in my life, I feel free. Free to be who I am and to do what I want without worrying about what others think. I'm happy."

She moved around the office finding it hard to stay in one place. Part of her appreciated that he cared enough to express his concern, but the other part of her was pissed off.

"I'm not living for all of you anymore. I'm living for me. I'm pursuing the things that make me happy. I want you to love me, continue being proud of me, and to respect me, but—"

"Sweetheart, none of that will ever change." He

gripped her shoulders, forcing her to look at him. "Okay, in hindsight, maybe I should've kept my mouth closed like your grandmother told me to, but I want so much for you kids. I don't ever want any of you to lower your standards, or your morals for anyone, especially a man."

"I know, and I understand that." And she did. Times had changed, but she knew her grandparents would always have their old school values which had served them well. Actually, their values had served all of them well. "Right now I'm okay with my decisions, and I haven't forgotten my home training."

Her grandfather smiled. "I know you haven't." He pulled her in for a hug. "But you know I had to say something."

"Yeah, I know."

He moved and sat behind his desk. "So when are you planning to leave and how long will you be gone?"

"We leave this weekend." Michael had planned to leave the day before but extended his trip to wait for her. "I'm not sure how long I'll be gone, but I'll stay in touch."

This whole idea was so unlike her. The straight-laced, dependable, never cause trouble or inconvenience to anyone Peyton Jenkins had changed. If anyone would have told her that she would take a leave of absence from a job she loved to follow a man to New York, she would have laughed in their faces.

But this was the new Peyton Jenkins. Anything was liable to happen.

*

Two weeks in New York and Peyton had fallen deeper in love with Michael and Manhattan. Maneuvering through the crowded streets to get to the M&M's store in Times Square, she felt like a native. She spent most of her time in Brooklyn, but this was her second time venturing to the city since arriving in town. Of course, Michael wasn't happy about her traipsing around town alone, but she couldn't let his fears dictate her comings and goings.

Peyton saw the store up ahead just as her cell phone rang. The ringtone signaling it was Michael.

"Hey, Babe." Peyton moved closer to a building to get out of the way of foot traffic.

"Peyton, I...out what," Michael said, the call breaking up. "Dyl...finan...tro."

"Michael, I can't understand you. You're breaking up. What about, Dylan?" She glanced at the phone when he didn't say anything more. The call had dropped. When she called back, she got his voicemail.

Peyton put her phone back into her handbag. What was Michael trying to tell her? Sounded like something about Dylan being in financial trouble, but she wasn't sure. What she didn't understand was why he couldn't wait and just tell her when he saw her.

Peyton had attended a late afternoon, Broadway show and Michael insisted on meeting her in Times Square for dinner. Since she wanted to pick up more M&M's to feed her and Michaela's addiction, he agreed to meet her at the store.

Peyton pulled open the glass door and strolled into the M&M's store feeling like a kid in a candy shop. She hadn't gone two feet before picking up a coffee mug filled with the delicious treats.

"Peyton."

She swung around and almost dropped the mug when she saw Dylan.

"Please just hear me out," Dylan begged, his hands out in front of him. Pleading eyes bore into her like she'd never seen before, desperation rang out in his voice.

Whatever was going on with him was serious.

"What are you doing here?" She glanced around, hoping Michael would be late. He was supposed to meet her there in ten minutes. The last thing she needed was for him to find Dylan near her. Another realization dawned on Peyton, and the hairs on the back of her neck stood at attention. "Why are you in New York and how did you even find me?"

"Can we talk?"

Michael had insisted that Dylan was up to no good, but she didn't want to believe him. She didn't think Dylan would cause her harm, but now she wasn't sure as she took a step back.

"Are you following me?" she whispered, thinking about the call she had just gotten from Michael.

"PJ, I just needed to talk to you. Please give me a couple of minutes to explain everything."

"We have nothing to talk about. The day you fu...screwed your assistant in our house was the day you lost the right to say anything to me. Whatever you have going on, I can't help you." She stepped around him, but he blocked her path.

"I'm in trouble," he spat and ran his hand over his low haircut. Still impeccably dressed, the only sign that he was distraught was the redness in his eyes and the creases in his forehead.

"You have one minute." They stepped farther into the store and over to the side out of the flow of traffic.

"I borrowed money from some very bad people and soon they will be trying to collect. I don't have the money." A year before their divorce, Dylan had started an import/export business. Considering how serious he was about his company, Peyton was surprised that he had gotten himself into a bind. She'd heard that he had purchased a huge home in the ritzy Indian Hill neighborhood and a number of luxury cars, but in the past, he never spent money he didn't have.

"Why would you borrow money from some loan shark or whoever?"

"I exhausted all of my credit and was expecting a contract to come through, but it's been delayed."

Michael had been right. Dylan did have an ulterior motive for seeking her out.

Peyton glanced at her cell phone, noting the time. Where are you, Michael? Rarely was he late, but maybe the meetings with his new clients had gone long.

"Dylan, I can't help you," she finally said.

"Yes, yes you can. Nobody saves money like you and I know you have $10,000 on hand."

"Whether I have it or not, I'm not giving it to you." Clearly he had lost his mind if he thought she was giving him anything.

"PJ, I promise I will pay you back." He touched her arm, and she jerked out of his grasp.

"You've promised me a lot in the past. Your promises mean nothing to me."

"My life is on the line, and you want to bring up my failures of the past? When did you become so heartless?"

Anger soared through her veins, and she took a step forward, standing face to face. "How dare you talk about heartless," her voice rasped a grainy whisper. "I gave my all to you and what did you do? You screwed another woman. So don't you dare come in here talking about me being heartless, you piece of sh…" She stopped talking when she noticed they were attracting attention. With so many children and families floating around the three-story building, it was not the place for this type of conversation.

"PJ, I'm so sorry for what I did to you. I was cocky, stupid and thought the world revolved around me. I know that now. Please don't let my past mistakes keep you from helping me. I've changed."

Peyton rolled her eyes and shook her head. "I don't care if you've changed. I'm done." She turned and walked away but stopped and glanced over her shoulder. "Lose my number and stop following me or I'll take out a restraining order."

"Wait." Dylan grabbed her arm. She tried pulling away, but his grip tightened. "Please, PJ, just hear me out."

"What the hell is wrong with you?" Michael snatched Dylan by the collar, seeming to have the strength of ten men as he lifted him and slammed his body into the wall. "Your ass is stupid enough to put your hands…"

"Oh no. Mike don't." Peyton pulled on the back of his shirt. He jerked his right shoulder sharply, throwing her off balance.

Peyton tripped. Her hand clipped the corner of an elaborate display, sending glass and candy crashing to the floor. A burning pain shot through her wrist and up her arm, taking her to her knees.

Her gaze connected with Michael's. The horror in his eyes stabbed her in the heart, knowing he would never forgive himself for this.

"Peyton!" He shoved Dylan away and headed toward her. Regret covering his face.

"Oh no you don't." Security intercepted him.

"Man, just let me make sure my woman is okay," Peyton heard Michael say.

"You should've thought of that in the first place." They pushed him back.

Sales clerks and shoppers came to her rescue while

security charged in from multiple directions. Ignoring the pain, all Peyton could think about was Michael. Memories of the bar fight story were at the forefront of her mind.

"I have to get to him," she said to no one in particular, chaos all around her. The pain in her hand worsened as she tried pushing her way through the massive crowd that had suddenly formed. She had to get to him. "Wait! This is all a misunderstanding."

Barely able to see over the tops of heads, she did see security shoving Dylan and Michael back.

"Ma'am, you're bleeding," an employee said. "Hey! I need some help over here."

"I have to go with my boyfriend. Michael!" she called out as a cop cuffed him. Michael met her gaze.

"Call Luke." She read his lips as they yanked on his arms and shoved him out the door.

Tears pricked the back of her eyes as she dug in the side of her bag, for her cell phone, finding the task difficult to maneuver with one hand.

"Ma'am, please sit down. The EMTs should be here shortly."

Unable to hold them back, tears flowed down her cheeks. "Please help me. I have to call my brother-in-law." With the woman's assistance, Peyton dialed.

"Hey, PJ," Luke answered on the second ring and Peyton sobbed.

"Luke, Michael's in trouble."

Chapter Nineteen

Hours later Peyton paced the length of Michael's living room, his mother sitting on the sofa wringing her hands, and his brother, Bailey sitting quietly next to her. The evening had been a nightmare, and it still wasn't over.

An ache twisted in Peyton's heart. She had shed more tears than she knew she had, especially when told that Michael didn't want her presence at the police station. Carlton had called an hour earlier to tell them the police had released Michael and that he was headed home.

Luke had contacted Bailey, and Rashon, Michael's youngest brother. They had shown up at the hospital just as Peyton was getting the cast put on. They both stayed until she was released. Bailey drove her to Michael's house, and Rashon left to pick up his girlfriend from work.

"I'm going to the kitchen. Do either of you need anything?" Bailey asked. When Peyton and Laura shook their heads, he left the room.

"I can't believe we're going through this again," Laura mumbled. "The last time almost broke Michael, almost destroyed him. He's never going to forgive himself for you getting hurt. He..." She stopped, and Peyton wondered what she was going to say.

"I'm sorry this happened." Peyton sat next to Laura, placing her good hand on the older woman's thigh. Peyton's left hand and wrist sported a cast thanks to two fractures in her hand. "I'm going to be fine, and Carlton said that Dylan wasn't pressing charges against Michael. We're all going to get through this. I love your son so much. Nothing is going to change that."

"You're sweet and just what my son needs. I only hope your love is enough."

"PJ!" Michaela yelled from upstairs. Despite insisting on waiting for her daddy to get home, she had fallen asleep a couple of hours ago.

When Michaela cried out again, Peyton stood. She wanted to know what Laura meant by her last comment but knew she needed to go to Michaela.

"I'll be right back."

Peyton calmed Michaela and waited until she drifted back to sleep before she headed toward the stairs. She stood frozen when she heard the front door open, her heart rate tripling. Michael had finally made it home.

"Where is she?" Michael asked in a rush, his voice traveling up the stairs. "Is she here?"

"She's here. She's checking on Michaela," Laura said. "Oh son, I'm so glad you're all right."

When Peyton made it down the stairs, she saw Bailey and Carlton first and then Michael, who was caught up in his mother's embrace.

Their gazes met. Her heart fluttered wildly. Peyton had never been this happy to see anyone in all of her life. It was as if a boulder had been lifted from her shoulders. Besides a little tired, he seemed fine physically. But his eyes told a different story. Weariness was evident as he rushed over to her.

Without a word, he pulled her against him tightly. His head buried in the crook of her neck, he held onto her as if they hadn't seen each other in months.

Tears flooded Peyton's eyes, and her throat tightened. Her emotions jumbled inside as she breathed in his scent, never wanting him to let her go.

"I'm sorry. Baby, I am so sorry," he repeated over and over next to her ear, his voice hoarse with emotion. He kissed the side of her head, his hold growing tighter.

"I'm just glad you're here and that you're okay," Peyton said knowing the night could have turned out differently, but was glad that everyone was okay.

Michael lifted his head, and Peyton knew the moment when his misty eyes spotted the bruise near her hairline. His features hardened in an instant. She had tried hiding the mark with her hair but apparently hadn't done a good job.

He stepped back, his chest heaving as he held her by the shoulders. His gaze strolled down her body but stopped at the cast on her hand.

"You said she was okay!" he growled at Bailey and dropped his arms from her shoulders.

"Hey, I told you what she told me to say!" Bailey snapped back.

"Shh, baby, I'm fine. See, I'm okay." She tried soothing Michael, her hand on his arm, but he stiffened under her touch.

"Dammit, Peyton! You have a cast on your hand and a bruise on the side of your head. And that's just what I can see. You're not fine!"

"That's enough, Michael!" His father's booming voice ricocheted off the walls immediately silencing Michael's rant.

Michael turned Peyton's face to get a better look. His eagle-eyed gaze traveled the length of her before returning his attention to her face. "Are you hurt anywhere else?"

"No, and the scar on my head doesn't even hurt," she lied. It stung, but she wasn't worried about a little discomfort. She grabbed Michael's hand and pulled him into the living room.

"I'm going to take your Mama home. Are you guys good?" Carlton asked, keys jingling in his hand.

"We'll be alright," Peyton said.

"I'm going to head out too," Bailey added.

"Thank you all for everything you did for us tonight." Peyton hugged them before seeing them out.

Michael refused to sit down, opting to stand near the fireplace.

"Carlton said there were no charges."

"Yeah, your ex-husband didn't nail me with assault charges." Michael closed his eyes and pinched the bridge of his nose, his forehead furrowed. Peyton glanced at the clock. Two a.m. and it was clear he was tired. By the grimace on his face, she also suspected he had a headache. "I'll just need to take care of the cost of damages at the store."

"I'll take care of that. This is all my fault any—"

"None of this is your fault!" he spat. "I saw him put his hands on you, and I lost it. Asking questions first never crossed my mind." His tone grew more annoyed with each word. For weeks, he thought Dylan was up to no good and had assumed the worst when seeing him.

Peyton slowly approached Michael, stopping a short distance in front of him. She kept her hands to herself, his agitation growing.

"You were right," Peyton said. "Dylan hunted me down because he wanted to borrow money. I'm sorry I didn't take the situation more seriously. I should have listened." Staring into Michael's intense eyes, she moved closer and wrapped her arms around his waist, laying her head against his chest. Relief flooded through her like a waterfall. He didn't push her away.

They stood holding each other. She didn't dare ask Michael where Dylan was and hoped her ex-husband had sense enough to stay away.

"Come on. Let's go to bed." Michael kissed the top of her head before releasing her.

Peyton waited by the stairs as he checked the doors and turned on the alarm system. When he approached her, his gaze went automatically to her cast and his jaw twitched. Instead of speaking, he held her uninjured hand and led her up the stairs.

Peyton sent up a silent prayer, thanking God for keeping Michael safe. They could get through this. As long as they were together, they could get through anything.

*

Early the next morning, Michael sat in the upholstered chair in his bedroom watching Peyton sleep. The night before was déjà vu. Six years ago, he had used poor judgment in dealing with a similar situation. Seeing Dylan grip Peyton's arm while she tried to pull away, made Michael see red. All he could remember thinking was that Peyton was in danger and he had to get to her. Yet, he had been the one to hurt her.

Across the room, Peyton yawned and stretched her arms up and out. With her eyes still closed, she reached over to his side of the bed and felt around before bolting upright. She squinted against the sunlight sneaking through the blinds, and rubbed her eyes.

"Hey," she finally said when she zoned in on him.

"Hey." He moved across the room and twisted the blinds closed. He sat on the edge of the bed, next to her, taking her all in. Even with her disheveled hair, she was still the most beautiful woman to him. They had come a long way since their first meeting on the plane, when she thought he was an arrogant ass.

Michael pushed her hair away from her forehead, avoiding the bruise. The back of his hand glided down the side of her face.

"How do you feel this morning?"

Peyton hesitated, searching his eyes as if trying to read his mood. She lifted the cast that covered her hand and wrist. "My arm aches a little, even though according to the x-rays there are no fractures, except for in my hand."

Anguish twisted around his heart for what his stupidity had put her through. What had he been thinking? Why hadn't he assessed the situation better before reacting?

Peyton glanced at the clock on the side table next to the bed. "It's only seven o'clock. Why are you up so early?"

Technically it wasn't early for him, but he couldn't sleep and had been up for hours. He had even carried his daughter over to his mother's house since he needed to talk to Peyton.

"Did you get any sleep?"

"A little." No need to tell her that he had sat up most of the night watching her sleep and thinking. Hearing her cry out in pain at the store, haunted him for the majority of the night.

"What's on your mind?"

"You. Us." He turned and bent forward, his elbows on his thighs. Michael struggled to swallow the lump that lingered in his throat. "We need to talk."

Peyton said nothing. Did she know what was coming? Did she know that he was about to do the hardest thing he had ever done in his life?

"Why do I have a feeling I'm not going to like this conversation?" She sat up straighter, adjusting the pillows behind her. "Michael, I know you're kicking yourself for what happened yesterday, but things happen. The situation just got a little out of hand."

"A little?" He shot off the bed. "Baby, your hand is broken because my stupid ass attacked someone. As a former cop, I know the ramifications of reacting before assessing the situation. As a person who has been in a similar situation before, I know how bad last night could have turned out. That was more than out of hand."

Michael turned away from her and rubbed the back of his neck. He had placed not only Peyton in danger, but everything he held dear could have been snatched away because he had gone off half-cocked after a man. Dylan could have easily pressed charges, but stated he shouldn't have touched Peyton.

Michael heard Peyton moving around. He had to talk to her. Part of him knew the decision he had come to about their future was for the best, but...

Peyton came up behind him and wrapped her arms around his waist, her head against his back. Michael placed his hands over hers. Feeling the hard cast on her hand made him relive the night all over again.

"I hate seeing you like this," she said, her voice muffled. "What can I do to make you feel better?"

Michael shook his head. "Nothing." He turned in her arms and held her tightly against his body, not wanting to let her go. Emotion clogged his throat, and his chest tightened.

Peyton lifted her head, and he stared into her concerned eyes. "I love you so damn much," he choked out and kissed her lips. The last time he felt as if his heart was crumbling into pieces like now, was when he had found his mother bloodied and unconscious because of Lewis. That same hopeless feeling gripped everything within him, refusing to let him breathe.

"I love you too." Peyton lifted up on her tiptoes and kissed him again, making what he had to say that much harder.

Breaking off the kiss, he cupped her face between his hands. "Please don't hate me."

Her brows dipped. "I could never hate you. Why would you even say something like that?" She caressed his cheek.

"I'm sending you home," he said. "Your flight leaves at two and Luke will pick you up at the airport once you land in Cincinnati."

Peyton pushed away from him, her eyes narrowed. "You're breaking up with me?"

I have to do this, he told himself.

"Yes."

"I'm not some child who you can just tell what to do or where to go. I'm not leaving!"

"Yeah, you are." Michael walked across the room and picked up her boarding pass from the small table next to the chair. Dropping the paper on the bed, he said, "I can't do this Peyton. I thought I could commit and do the whole relationship thing and live a normal life, but I can't. I can't risk something like last night happening again. When I walked in and saw Dylan, I..."

Michael shook his head, his words clogging his throat. He squeezed his eyes closed. His fists balled at his sides.

"I can't leave, Michael." Peyton's voice cracked, tears

trekked down her face. "I won't. You have never done anything to hurt me. This generational curse you speak of, I haven't seen proof of it based on the way you've treated Michaela and me."

She wiped furiously at her tears, but they came faster, breaking Michael's heart even more.

"I'm so sorry you grew up in an abusive home, but in my heart, I know that would never happen to us. It would never happen in our home. You would *never* put your hands on me like that, and I'm not giving up on us. I love you too much to let you go."

His mother had been like that when he was growing up, thinking that her love for his father would be enough to save him. Even with Lewis going to Alcoholics Anonymous meetings, nothing changed. If anything, their lives got worse. It wasn't until Lewis beat her to within an inch of her life that she finally said, no more.

Michael didn't want that for Peyton. She was the sweetest, most giving person he knew. He didn't want her to have to deal with his overprotectiveness. And he didn't want to risk her going through all that his mother had experienced.

"A car will be here to pick you up at—"

"Did you hear me?" She pounded against his chest with a closed fist. "I'm not leaving!"

He grabbed her hand and brought it to his lips. "You have to, Peyton. What if the type of anger I felt when seeing your ex-husband's hands on you transforms, and somehow screws up my head? What if I come after you? What if I put my hands on you?" The thought twisted in his gut. He didn't trust himself. He couldn't take the chance. Michael released her hand and stepped back. "If you don't leave today, then I'm leaving."

Peyton reared back as if she'd been slapped, her eyes

growing big. "What are you talking about?"

"If you don't leave here, I'll take my daughter and leave. I won't return until I know that you're safe in Cincinnati."

Her mouth dropped opened. "This is crazy, Michael. Why are you doing this? Why are you walking away from what we have, what we've built?" She cried, stomping her feet, frustration bouncing off of her. She paced the room like a caged animal, a look of disbelief on her face and pain in her eyes.

"I have to do this, Peyton, and I need you to go home." Despite his words, he didn't want her to leave. The reality of knowing he might never see her again was killing him. "Just know that I love you."

"Then don't do this," she said, her voice a hoarse whisper. Most of the fight seemed to have left her. "Please don't do this."

Michael walked out of the bedroom, closing the door behind him. Even when she swung the door open and ran down the stairs after him, he kept moving until he was out the front door, no destination in mind.

Chapter Twenty

Peyton roamed around her partially vacant home feeling lost. A month had passed since she'd left New York and there were moments when she still couldn't believe she and Michael were over. He loved her. She knew he loved her. If only he could conquer his fears.

"It's over. Move on," she mumbled to herself. She'd spoken the words many times, by now they should've been engrained in her head. But her heart couldn't let him go, wouldn't let him go.

Nick, bumping around upstairs, grabbed her attention. He and some of her other cousins came over earlier to help move her furniture and some boxes to a storage unit. Moving on from Michael was harder than it had been with Dylan. She had played around with the idea of selling her home months ago and knew now she had to. She couldn't stay in the house. Too many memories, good and bad. She was moving in with Jada and Zach, who were traveling so much, they were rarely home. She didn't plan to stay with them long, just long enough to decide her next steps.

Peyton glanced around the lower level, her heart aching. Between Dylan's betrayal and Michael's issues, she was giving up on men. Clearly she didn't know how to pick one. What she wasn't giving up on was having a family. She didn't need a man for that and had looked into adopting.

Michael's intense eyes sparked inside her mind. No, she didn't need a man, but there was one she really wanted.

Peyton swiped at the tears rolling down her face, surprised there were any left. She didn't know which was worse, being lonely or being broken hearted. Heck at the moment she was both.

"Stop. It's over. Move on," she said again just as Nick bounded down the stairs carrying a box. He slowed and looked at her, a frown on his face.

"Dang, Peyton, it's been over a month. Are you sure you don't want me and the boys to go to New York and kick his ass?"

He said it with a straight face which made Peyton chuckle. "No. Craig, Zack, Jerry, Ben Junior, and your twin already offered. Even Luke is willing." Luke seemed to take the break up just as hard as she had, saying he thought for sure Michael had finally chosen love over fear. He didn't know how to help his friend get over the anxiety of possibly being an abuser. Luke had told her that Michael did agree to see a counselor and felt it was helping, but he also said that whenever he mentioned Peyton's name, Michael shut him down.

"Are you sure?" Nick persisted. "Because if you're going to keep the waterworks going like you've been, we have to do something."

Peyton shook her head wondering why she was even listening to this nonsense. "I'm sure." She was probably saving all of them a butt whooping. Michael would pummel them. Some of her cousins might have been bigger and in some cases taller, but Michael was strong, arrogant, and had a serious chip on his shoulder. Despite those faults, she still believed he was perfect for her.

"This is why I will never fall in love," Nick said and set the box down near the front door. "It's not worth the stress."

"Yeah, you say that now. Trust me, when the right woman comes along, you won't know what hit you. All your stupid talk about being a bachelor until the day you die will fly right out the door. I can't wait to say I told you so."

"Yeah, whatever. Anyway, I think we have everything loaded in my truck. The guys are almost done unloading the stuff they took to your storage unit."

"That's good. Thanks. Oh and next weekend I'm heading to Vegas. Can you be the contact person for my realtor if needed?" Peyton had decided to continue her leave of absence from work. She figured she might as well do the traveling she had put off before Michael came along.

"Come on, Peyton. Can't you get someone else? I'll probably be putting in long hours at work, especially since you've abandoned us. Get someone else to babysit your real—"

"Hello?" A voice sang out with two quick knocks on the door.

"In here, Sumeera," Peyton said, recognizing the voice of one of her best friends who happened to be her realtor.

Peyton almost burst out laughing at the look on Nick's face when Sumeera stepped into the living room. Wearing a tight red blouse with a low neckline and jeans that fit like a second skin, accented with high heels the color of her shirt, she looked as if she had just stepped off the cover of *Vogue*.

Nick's mouth hung open, but he quickly closed it. In his defense, Sumeera was a beautiful woman who had the same effect on every man she met.

"Hey, PJ." Sumeera hugged her tight. "It looks like you're really serious about selling." She gazed around the mostly empty room. "I'll take some pictures and then list your house in the morning. I think the place is going to sell quickly."

Nick cleared his throat, wiping his hands on his jeans. Peyton started to ignore him, but with the pitiful facial expression he was sporting, she figured she'd put him out of his misery.

"I'm sorry, Sumeera, this is my cousin, Nick. Nick, this is my friend and *realtor*."

"Nice to meet you," he said shaking Sumeera's hand.

"Sumee, I was going to have Nick be your contact person, but he—"

"Is happy to be at your service," Nick jumped in.

Peyton rolled her eyes.

"Let me show you around. Nick held his bent arm to Sumeera, and of course, she accepted his offer, a sweet smile on her face. Little did Nick know that she probably knew the house better than him. She had stayed there for months while her house was being renovated a couple of years ago.

Not known for being with one woman for too long, Nick had a good heart and could use a woman like Sumeera to show him what he was missing by not committing.

A shiver ran through Peyton at her last thought.

He's nothing like Michael. Michael could commit if he

just gave himself permission and quit being afraid of something that would never happen.

*

"You are not your father, Michael! How many times do I have to tell you that? You are not Lewis!" his mother yelled from the other side of the kitchen counter. She'd been drilling those words into him since he'd been old enough to date. "If anything, you're more like Carlton than anyone. You're a wonderful man and a loving father."

"I might not be my father, but—"

"But nothing. You have to believe that you're a good, loving man. Carlton and I saw to that. I believe in generational curses, but in this case, that curse has been broken starting with you! None of my boys are abusers, and none of you ever will be!" She slapped her hand on the marbled counter top.

Michael stood and strolled over to her, not wanting her to break down into tears the way she had the night he was arrested. Carlton had already warned him that if he made her cry again, he was going to kick his ass. And Michael believed him.

"Calm down, Mom." He said wrapping his arm around her shoulder.

She shook out of his hold. "I will not calm down until you start hearing me!" She busied herself at the stove. "I want you to have a good woman who will love you unconditionally, and I think you had that with Peyton. Yes, you have a short fuse when you think the women in your life are in danger, but who wouldn't? No real man would stand by and watch a woman get mistreated by another man."

That might be true, but Michael didn't want a repeat of the night Peyton ended up with a broken hand. He didn't know if she was still in a cast, but some nights when he closed his eyes, the day at the M&M's store looped through his mind. When Peyton cried out in pain, his heart lurched. And the fact that he couldn't get to her tore him up inside.

Michael leaned against the counter and reached for his coffee. He'd worked hard to put that night behind him, to move on from Peyton. Neither was easy to do. A day hadn't gone by that he didn't think of her, or yearn for her. And even though he'd been tempted to call Peyton every morning and night, he reframed. Thinking about her was hard enough, he couldn't handle hearing her voice.

Michael watched in silence as his mother whipped up a batch of cupcakes for him and Michaela. His daughter hadn't taken the news of Peyton leaving well, but cupcakes and keeping her busy were a good distraction. M&M's used to work, but lately, she hadn't wanted the sweet treats not that Michael was surprised. The snack was her and Peyton's thing.

Michael sipped his black coffee. The day Peyton left, he contacted a therapist that Luke had recommended. Swallowing his pride, he'd been meeting with the woman twice a week. Though doubts popped into his head periodically about his progress, he was finally winning against his inner demons.

"Peyton is the best thing that ever happened to you, and I can't believe you still haven't gone after her."

He couldn't believe it either.

"Michael, you have to go and get her. You can't let a woman like that walk out of your life. True love only comes around once."

"Even if I thought she would give me another chance, Peyton is way out of my league." It was a wonder she'd given him the time of day in the first place.

His mother waved him off. "Don't give me that. Go and find her before it's too late. Find her before someone else comes along and claims what was meant for you. If you still love her, go and get her."

∗

Peyton handed Jada the rest of the dishes. She thought for sure she would get out of cleanup duty after Sunday brunch since she still had a cast on her hand, but no such luck. It had been six weeks, and she was finally getting the cast off the next morning.

Peyton dried a glass bowl, awkwardly balancing the dish against her good hand to place it in the cabinet with the other serving dishes. This was the last Sunday brunch before her trip to Vegas and then on to Los Angeles. She considered canceling the trip again, but if she ever wanted to get her life back on track, she had to move on.

"These are the last two platters." Jada set the dishes into the soapy water. "We need to find an industrial size dishwasher for this house because doing all of these dishes is getting old."

"What we need to do is start rotating the guys into the clean-up schedule. They all know how to cook. Now they need to practice cleaning." Peyton dried another bowl, careful not to get her cast wet.

"That's perfect. I'll work on Gramma to get that going while you're out of town." Jada rinsed the platter. "I've been thinking about something else," she said, her voice low as if ready to share a secret.

"What?"

"You're a take-charge person." Jada placed her hands on her hips, her mouth twisted with disdain. "Why aren't you taking charge of your personal life? You're like taking a backseat, waiting for something to happen."

"What are you talking about?" Peyton frowned, her hand hovering near the open cabinet door.

"I can't take any more of your moping around. Maybe this trip will help you get your head together, but I don't think so. If you know Mike's the man for you, why have you given up on him?"

Peyton patted her hands on a dry towel, giving Jada her full attention. Since marrying Zack, Jada had changed. She was still selfish at times, but she had grown more considerate over the past year and a half.

"Hear me out before you tell me to shut up and quit being nosy."

Peyton laughed. Normally she would say something like that, but right now, Peyton wanted to hear any ideas Jada had that might help her, and Michael find their way back to each other.

"When it comes to the family business, you're the master at making deals happen. We have watched you convince clients that Jenkins & Sons is their best choice, and you guarantee them a hundred percent satisfaction. Why not use your negotiating skills with Michael? Why not convince him that he is never going to find another woman as great as you?"

Peyton's brows shot up and she leaned back. A tug of emotion pulled at her heartstrings.

Jada placed a glass bowl in the dishwater. "Don't act so surprised. You know you're the total package. Michael knows it too. He's just too...too stupid to admit to himself that he's never going to be happy without you."

Peyton leaned her hip against the kitchen counter, tossing Jada's words around in her mind. Peyton always went after what she wanted, but it had never crossed her mind to pursue Michael. Bidding on construction projects was different than forcing someone to want to be with her.

"I can't, Jada." Peyton took a breath. She'd been doing good keeping Michael out of her thoughts, but now that ache in her heart returned. "My Mom once told me that if a man loved me enough, he would pursue me. She said I'm the prize. I truly believe that. Michael has to deal with his issues and then if he and I are meant to be together, he has to come to me. Not the other way around."

A slow smile spread across Jada's lips. "Well alright now. You go Ms. Thang."

Martina strolled into the kitchen carrying Janay. "PJ, we're getting ready to head out. Do you want to say bye to your goddaughter?"

"You know I do." She reached for the baby and that tightness she always felt around her heart whenever she held Janay, returned. "Hey, my little sweetie-pie," she said in baby talk, kissing Janay's chubby cheeks. The baby gave a quick smile and wiggled in Peyton's arms. She couldn't believe how fast her little goddaughter was growing.

"You girls forgot a few dishes," Katherine Jenkins said. Toni followed behind her carrying plates.

Jada huffed. "Where did that stuff come from? I checked the dining room and downstairs for dirty dishes."

"Grampa and Uncle Thomas ate in the study. They're still talking and hadn't thought to bring the dishes in here," Toni said, placing the small pile on the counter.

"At this rate we're never going to get out of here," Jada mumbled, trying to wedge more dishes into the dishwasher. "Gramma, it's time for the guys to start helping clean up. We should establish a new rule. You eat. You clean."

"That's a good idea, Jada." Their grandmother poured herself a glass of ice tea. "You can help me come up with a new schedule."

Jada gave Peyton the side eye, and Peyton smirked, nuzzling the baby's neck to keep from laughing out loud.

"Peyton, someone's here to see you." Peyton turned at the sound of her mother's voice, and her heart stuttered. She nearly dropped to her knees, her emotions strangled her vocal cords.

"Hello, Peyton."

The women in her family dropped back and parted like the Red Sea when Michael walked into the kitchen.

"Close your mouth girl and give me my baby before you drop her." Martina lifted Janay from Peyton's arms.

"Alright girls, let's give them some privacy." Their grandmother hustled everyone out of the kitchen.

Martina nudged Michael on her way out. "It's about damn time you found your way back to her. I was about ready to hunt you down myself."

Peyton's heart cracked a little when Michael flashed that crooked grin that she'd missed and shook his head at Martina.

"Well, well, well," Jada said from behind Peyton. "If it isn't the—"

"Let's go, Jada. Now," her grandmother said from the doorway.

"Dang," she grumbled and tossed the dishtowel on the kitchen island before leaving.

Now it was just the two of them. Peyton had no clue what to say. She still found it hard to believe that he was standing in her grandparent's kitchen. How many times had she dreamt about this moment? About what it would be like if she ever saw him again. Touched him again.

"I should have called first, but I thought you wouldn't take my call."

Michael's intense brown-eyed gaze pierced her heart,

making every part of her quiver. He moved closer and a whimper crawled up her throat. Her hands eased to her mouth as a burst of emotions came rushing back. Tears clouded her eyes.

"I'm sorry. Baby, I'm so sorry." Michael stopped a foot in front of her and reached out, but dropped his arm before making contact. "There hasn't been a day that I haven't thought of you."

He blew out a ragged breath and ran a hand over his head and down the back of his neck. Peyton swiped at her tears, watching him pace in front of her. She wanted so bad to reach out and hold him, assure him that they were going to be okay, but she didn't. He needed to tell her what was in his heart, and she needed to hear it.

"My mother has told me more times than I can count that I am not my father or my grandfather." Michael kept moving, looking away from Peyton. "Even though deep in my heart, I knew this was true, I carried their sins right here." He stopped and pointed to his chest when his gaze met hers.

"Oh, Michael," Peyton sobbed unable to stop herself as she felt his pain deep inside.

He stepped closer. "My mother also reminded me that not only am I nothing like them, but I am also capable of love. I am worthy of love. She told me that I am worthy of you. That was something I struggled with since meeting you."

"You are." Peyton took a step toward him, and he closed the distance, pulling her into his arms, holding her tight. "You are worthy," she said against his neck, soaking up his warmth and strength. The familiar scent of his cologne wrapped around her, bringing her a level of peace she hadn't felt in a long time.

"I love you," he mumbled against her hair, holding her

tighter. "I love you so damn much. I don't want to live without you. Baby, I can't live without you."

"I love you too, and I've missed you."

Michael leaned back and framed her face within his large hands, wiping her tears away with the pad of his thumbs.

"For over a month, I've been in family counseling. It's helped a lot. So much so that I reclaim my life, a life I want to share with you. Peyton, I will never touch you in anger. I'm working on my overprotectiveness. And I promise to ask questions before I react to any situation. Can you forgive me for the way I've handled our relationship? Give me another chance? I will change to be the man you want."

Peyton fisted her hands in the front of his shirt. "Michael, I don't want you to change. You are the man I want. I love you. I love you just the way you are. I've always known you would never hurt me. I'm relieved you finally know that for yourself."

He lowered his mouth to hers. The gentleness of his kiss made Peyton weak in the knees. She kissed him back, deeply, hoping he could feel how much she loved and cherished him. Her whole body responded when he deepened the kiss, squeezing her against him as if planning never to let go. Peyton dreamt of this moment. The moment when she and Michael were back together, and all felt right in her world.

"There's one other thing," Michael mumbled against her lips before stepping back. He dug into his pocket, pulling out a black velvet pouch. "I want us to make this official." He bent to one knee, and Peyton's breath caught, her hand resting against her pounding heart. "I'm not good with fancy words, but I can tell you what I feel. I love you, Peyton. It wasn't until you were gone did I realize how embedded you are in my heart. These last few weeks without you have been the hardest. I can't go another day without knowing if you'll be my wife."

Michael held up the oval garnet surrounded by diamonds in a platinum setting. "Will you marry me?"

Peyton's gaze bounced from the ring, sparkling under the kitchen lights, to Michael, his eyes filled with so much hope.

"Give me a chance to show you how much I love you. I swear I'll never leave you, nor will I ever push you away again. Peyton Jenkins, please say you'll be my wife. Will you marry me?"

Peyton nodded. Tears of joy blurred her vision as she wrapped her arms around his neck and he stood tall holding her in his arms.

"Yes. Yes, I'll marry you!"

Epilogue

Four Days Later

"I can't believe I let you talk me into eloping," Michael said as he and Peyton lounged in the huge, soaking tub in a Las Vegas hotel room. Bubbles surrounded them as they bathed by candlelight, a bottle of non-alcoholic champagne and glasses sat near the tub.

"You have to admit. It was a great idea." Peyton turned slightly, and they shared a noisy kiss. She couldn't remember the last time she was this happy. As a little girl, she had believed in fairy tales, believed that the princess always got her prince. After Dylan had betrayed her, cynicism settled in and though she wanted a second chance at love, she never thought it would happen. Then Michael came along.

"It was an awesome idea, but I'm afraid I might be a bad influence on you. This idea sounded more like it should've come from me instead of you." He ran the sponge down the front of her body and Peyton's eyes fluttered closed as a peace settled over her.

Sunday, after informing every one of their

engagement, she and Michael spent the rest of that evening discussing their future. Michael agreed to travel with her to Vegas, saying he had missed her so much. He wanted to be wherever she was. When asked when she wanted to get married, Peyton told him she didn't want a long engagement.

The eloping idea hadn't come to her until early that morning, their fourth day in Vegas after passing by a wedding chapel. At first, Michael insisted on giving her the fairytale wedding, but Peyton shot the idea down. She'd already had the dream wedding when she married Dylan, and their life together disintegrated. An elaborate wedding didn't guarantee a happy marriage. Getting married in a little chapel on the Las Vegas Strip was so unlike the old Peyton. The new Peyton knew this was just how she wanted to start her life with Michael. Unpredictable. Unpretentious. Simple, like the love they shared.

She opened her eyes when Michael reached for his glass of champagne.

"You know, I liked the old Peyton, the one I used to banter with when we first met. But I'm feelin' this new you too." He wiggled behind her and nuzzled her neck, eliciting a laugh.

"Yeah, I like the new me too."

*

Michael took another sip from his glass, enjoying the soft jazz floating from the iPod speaker, still trippin'. He was a married man. Peyton had shocked the hell out of him when she told him she wanted a Vegas wedding. He would have married her anywhere, anytime. His only goal — make her happy.

Asking Peyton to be his wife was the best decisions he'd ever made. Before arriving in Cincinnati, he informed his family, including Michaela, of his intentions. Once Peyton said yes, they Facetimed his family to share the news. When Michaela started making plans for her and Peyton, Michael knew he had made the right decision for both him and his daughter.

"So Boss Lady, are you sure you want to change your Los Angeles travel plans? I can take a few more days off. Michaela is perfectly fine with my parents."

"Positive, but still plan on taking the days off. We have some logistics to work out before I relocate."

Michael nodded. When he planned to propose to her, he had prepared himself for the possibility that she would want them to live in Cincinnati. Though he loved New York, he could work anywhere, and would leave in a heartbeat if she wanted to live somewhere else. Michael already knew from their brief separation that he or his home wasn't the same without her. He was never letting her go.

He set his glass down on the wide ledge surrounding the tub and wrapped his arms around Peyton's naked body.

"Mrs. Cutter, are you falling asleep on me?"

"I love it when you call me Mrs. Cutter and no I'm not asleep." She sat up and turned to face him, her bare breasts taunting him as she straddled his lap. "In fact, I think we should climb out, dry off, and test out that huge bed again."

"Mmm, I like the way you think." Michael captured her lips in a passionate kiss that stoked the flames within him. God, he loved this woman. "I have a better idea," he mumbled against her mouth. "Why don't we forget the bed and start working on giving Michaela a little brother or a sister right here. Right now."

"Ohhh," she purred when he slid inside of her sweet

heat. "That's the best idea yet."

***

If you enjoyed this book by Sharon C. Cooper,
consider leaving a review.

About the Author

Award-winning and bestselling author, Sharon C. Cooper, is a romance-a-holic - loving anything that involves romance with a happily-ever-after, whether in books, movies, or real life. Sharon writes contemporary romance, as well as romantic suspense and enjoys rainy days, carpet picnics, and peanut butter and jelly sandwiches. She's been nominated for numerous awards and is the recipient of an Emma Award for Romantic Suspense of the Year 2015 (Truth or Consequences), Emma Award - Interracial Romance of the Year 2015 (All You'll Ever Need), and BRAB (book club) Award - Breakout Author of the Year 2014. When Sharon is not writing or working, she's hanging out with her amazing husband, doing volunteer work or reading a good book (a romance of course). To read more about Sharon and her novels, visit www.sharoncooper.net

Connect with Sharon Online:

Website: http://sharoncooper.net
Facebook:
http://www.facebook.com/AuthorSharonCCooper21?re
f=hl
Twitter: https://twitter.com/#!/Sharon_Cooper1
Subscribe to her blog:
http://sharonccooper.wordpress.com/
Goodreads:
http://www.goodreads.com/author/show/5823574.Shar
on_C_Cooper
Pinterest: https://www.pinterest.com/sharonccooper

Other Titles by Sharon C. Cooper:

Coming Soon: Jenkins & Sons Construction Series

Jenkins Family Series (Contemporary Romance)
Best Woman for the Job (Short Story Prequel)
Still the Best Woman for the Job (book 1)
All You'll Ever Need (book 2)
Tempting the Artist (book 3)
Negotiating for Love – (book 4)
Seducing the Boss Lady – (book 5)

Reunited Series (Romantic Suspense)
Blue Roses (book 1)
Secret Rendezvous (Prequel to Rendezvous with Danger)
Rendezvous with Danger (book 2)
Truth or Consequences (book 3)
Operation Midnight (book 4)

Stand Alones
Something New ("Edgy" Sweet Romance)
Legal Seduction (Harlequin Kimani – Contemporary Romance)
Sin City Temptation (Harlequin Kimani – Contemporary Romance)
A Dose of Passion (Harlequin Kimani – Contemporary Romance)
Model Attraction (Harlequin Kimani – Contemporary Romance)

Made in the USA
Lexington, KY
20 July 2016